HO

OF THE DRUG

GAME:

AZUL &

JUSTICE

C. WILSON

Copyright © 2023 C Wilson

Published by Tina J Presents

FOLLOW C. WILSON ON SOCIAL MEDIA

Instagram: @authorcwilson

Facebook: Celeste Wilson

TikTok: @celestialcosmeticsatl

Twitter: @Authorcwilson_

Join my reading group on Facebook:

Cecret Discussionz

Follow my reading group on Instagram:

@CecretDiscussionz

Tell me what you think of this story in a customer review.

Thank you,

-xoxo-

C. Wilson

AZUL AND JUSTICE'S MUSIC

PLAYLIST

Martin & Gina, Polo G

I Been Drinking, Future

Red Ruby Da Sleeze, Nicki Minaj

Painting Pictures, Superstar Pride

No Love, J.K. Mac

Skrubs, Lil Durk

Back Home, Trey Songz ft. Summer Walker

Worth It, Young Thug

Coming Clean, Lil Durk

Banking On Me, Gunna

Hard For The Next, Moneybagg Yo ft. Future

C. WILSON

In A Minute, Lil Baby

Slatt Bizness, Slimelife Shawty

MINE, Beyonce ft. Drake

You Were Right, Lil Uzi Vert

Snooze, SZA

CHAPTER 1

JUSTICE

I used the back of my hand to wipe the snot from under my nose as I sniffled. I couldn't stop the salty trails from falling. This was the shit that I hated; he was never here. I carefully walked out of the room, making sure not to step in any of the blood that covered the floors. I knew that once Azul got here, he would call for the cleaner; and he sure did have a lot to clean. I closed the room door behind me and slowly walked towards the living room to have a seat and wait for him. I stared at a blank spot on the wall as my mind drifted to the robbery that had just occurred a few hours ago...

"I shouldn't have to talk to y'all dumb asses more than once. It's simple... hand me the bag so that I can count what y'all made and take y'all re-up. Where the fuck is the confusion in what I just said? Y'all little niggas wanna sit

here and chit chat!" I barked as I looked at Azul's two new workers that stood in front of me.

Our crew was small and ran efficiently because of it. Doley was second in command, under Azul of course, and he always rolled by himself, hence the nickname. It had been that way since we were in middle school. So, when it came to recruiting, he never added new niggas to the team. That left Azul with the task of finding workers. I offered my help with expansion, but Azul loved to micromanage. He had a thing for pulling in young niggas and putting them on the team. It made no difference to me because they were money-hungry and hard workers that always moved their product in half of the time that they were given.

"My apologies boss lady," one of them said to me as he took the duffle bag off one of the 6 by 8 tables that stood inside the vacant bedroom.

Knock, knock… knock, knock, knock.

Recognizing the methodical code knock at the door, I nodded my head towards the front for one of the boys to go see who was knocking. Within minutes, I heard a bunch of commotion.

"Close that door, hurry up!" I said to the other worker in the room with me.

Reaching into my purse that sat on one of the empty tables, I pulled my Sig from out of it and cocked it back quickly. Before the young boy could close the door, it was kicked open with a force that knocked him on his ass.

"Stay the fuck down little nigga!" one of the masked men said to the worker that was attempting to get up.

It was three other men in ski masks that slowly poured into the room. That's when I knew I had no wins. I was a great shot but not good enough to take out all four of them without one of them killing me. Still, I thought of all of the possibilities of how this would play out if I did take that

shot.

"Put that cute little gun down baby girl," the one that

was calling the shots said to me as he pointed his pistol my

way.

I slowly dropped my gun to the floor. The silencer on

the end of his snub let me know that he came here to kill.

Instantly, a hollow feeling came to the pit of my stomach

when he shot our worker that still sat on the floor in the head

without hesitation or remorse. His eyes then trained on me.

"To kill you... or not to kill you? Which one love?"

he asked as he waved the gun in front of me, taunting me.

With a father that used to run the streets before his

demise, I was born into this lifestyle. That's how Azul and I

clicked all of those years ago. I saw the vision of where he

was trying to go and jumped on for the ride. Daddy always

taught me to have that poker face; it was the look of steel that saved me a lot on the streets. I was just silently praying that it would save me this time.

"Do what you gotta do," I said as I stared into his eyes.

I wasn't about to show him any kind of weakness. There was a familiarity to those pupils that was nagging me as we stared at one another. He let silence fill the room as he stared deep into my eyes. I scrunched my eyebrows in thought as I tried to think of who the fuck this nigga was. I blinked away quickly when he broke our stare down.

"Y'all get those bags," he said to the three other men that stood aimlessly around the room. Immediately, they followed his order and cleaned us the fuck out.

"Tell Zoo he knows who to come to see. The only reason I'm not gone smoke ya pretty ass is to deliver that message, and you are fucking pretty."

Something about his voice was familiar too. I just couldn't put my finger on who the fuck he was. He blew a kiss my way and slowly backed out of the room, following behind his team. I stood still with a face of stone until I heard the front door close. As soon as it did, I ugly girl cried. Although I tried my best to prepare myself for situations like this, I wasn't ready to go. I thanked God for sparing me...

"Yo, what the fuck!"

Azul's deep tone broke me from my daze. He walked into the house on his phone. "Yeah, get here now Doley, and bring the cleaner with you. It's a mess," he said as he stepped over the broken front door pieces and the dead body of one of his recruits. He ended the call and just stared at me. Those bushy caterpillar brows dented in anger. When I made eye contact with those deep brown orbs, his face frowned a bit.

"Come here Ma," he said as he held his strong tatted arms out for me.

11

I ran to him and fell into his embrace. My small stature fell easily into his robust 6'5 frame. Being his Queen Pin was going to break me one day, I felt it and I was sure he did too. He knew I was tough and about this life, but he also knew that I was an emotional female as well. I would blow a nigga head off and then cry later while washing the blood from my hands. I always did what I had to do, but that didn't mean that my conscience didn't feel troubled afterward.

It's hard to understand the light if you had never been in the dark and, in the shadows of misery, Azul and I blossomed. Many times, he stood behind me in my shower and washed me clean as the crimson color of blood from me catching yet another body pooled at our feet and circled down the drain. I just knew that when I died that I would be getting an express ticket to hell. I knew what my fate was, and I even took little small precautions to prepare myself like washing in steaming hot water. I had too many bodies on my hands to ever think that I was getting that escalator ride up top. Over the years, it did soften my hard exterior.

It took a lot to take a life and if anybody out here was saying it didn't, then they were just trying to seem hard. Azul understood that because every time he took a life, I saw a change in him. I appreciated him for understanding the soft side of me, but the nigga was never on the front line with me during war. Although he did show up immediately after, I needed him while I was standing ten toes down. Instead of being back-to-back with me in the trenches, he was always tending to his cleaning business or with his wife.

"What the fuck happened?" he asked in a shocked tone. We let go of our embrace, and he followed me outside because I needed some air.

"Some niggas just ran up in here when the new niggas came and brought the money. It could have been a set up because they knew the knock Zoo. How else could they know it? Those young niggas you hired turned snake and they ass got clipped for it," I said as I shook my head and started digging in my purse for my THC pen. My nerves were shot, and I needed to quickly calm down.

"Damn, did the niggas say anything?" Azul asked as he stroked his thick beard that fell about three inches from his chiseled jawline.

The streetlight shining above us had his deep chocolate skin glistening. I could tell that he was annoyed by the way his jaw tightened and his biceps involuntarily flexed under the rim of his white t-shirt.

"Yeah, they said you know who to holler at. So, who was it, Zoo? I thought you said you had shit on lock. You're the one that said nobody could fuck with us. You make it seem like gang is untouchable when tonight proves that to be a muthafucking lie," I spat slickly.

I was livid about this robbery. We had been hit before but it never ended in bloodshed, and I was never personally there when our other trap houses got raided. Being there for this one felt like the get back had to be personal. I didn't like how I felt touchable. It was an unsettling feeling and I hated not feeling safe. Azul knew that when I didn't feel safe, someone had to be put in the ground for it.

"It could really only be one nigga, Ma. It had to be Travis and his crew," he said.

Trav and Zoo's beef was something that one may call everlasting. It all started when Azul, me and David, better known as Doley, were in our senior year of high school. When Azul's mother got sick, it changed him. He had always been a bad boy, but he had never been a street nigga. Trauma and survival instincts quickly altered that for him. Around Brooklyn, Zoo quickly became the man known for slinging grade a fish scale. He got in good with the Mexican cartel by dating a Mexican girl in our school, Isabella.

She was a quiet girl in school, but the power behind her was massive because she was the plug's niece. When he started getting product and selling, Doley and I joined in without a second thought. With pushing drugs all over East New York, we needed more people than the *Troubled Trio* that I used to call us. Taking Trav under the wing was completely Zoo's decision. I always knew that something was funny with his ass. If Zoo would buy a fresh pair of kicks or a new whip, here came Trav with the same pair of sneakers or the same model car just a few weeks later because he never had the funds to cash out on whatever item right then and there. I felt his animosity towards Zoo immediately. Back then, I kept my distance because one thing I couldn't stand was a snake ass nigga. The vibe he gave off was envy, and I knew that nothing good would come from him remaining on the team.

It only got worse when later down the line, Trav tried to pursue me. I guess he saw me as fair game because Doley always had a chick on his arm and Azul was already dating Isabella. Their relationship was strictly business but only Doley and I knew that. Well, that's how Azul put it to us. So, I would deny Trav's advances because I knew that he was only giving them because he had no idea that I had already belonged to someone else.

They later had a falling out over money, which led to them fighting and Zoo beating the shit out of Travis. Outside in front of everybody, he rag-tagged his ass and, as a man, I knew that Trav's pride would be forever flawed because of it. That situation led to Trav trying to step on Zoo's toes every chance he got and vice versa. After taking another puff from my THC pen, I exhaled slowly.

"It's time for you to knock this nigga off the map, Pa. He has been playing with us for far too long and tonight… tonight was the last straw."

Azul twisted his mouth like he wanted to say something back to me, but he didn't. He was a meticulous man, so I already knew that he had some form of payback brewing in his mind. Instead of offering me a response, he just wrapped his arm around my waist and pulled me closer to him. He kissed the top of my head gently and inhaled my natural scent.

"I'm glad you're okay Ma."

I stood still in his embrace and, as the light summer breeze blew, his cologne invaded my nostrils. Baccarat Rouge 540 was his signature scent on a chill day, and I was obsessed with the fragrance because of him.

"Stay the night with me," I said in a whisper.

He sighed before letting go of me. "I can't Ma, not tonight."

Fucking shitting me! I thought as I took another puff of my pen. His staying the night with me had become less

18

frequent. *When home life calls, I guess,* I thought silently to myself as I inwardly despised his wife. He had an image to uphold and keeping that prissy Mexican bitch happy kept the money coming, so I never complained. I was understanding of the ultimate sacrifice he had made. It kept money flowing for the team, so he probably would never hear me complain about that.

"Sorry it took me a little minute to get here; it's traffic on Atlantic Ave," Doley said as he and Zoo engaged in the gangsta shake-up. He gave me a hug before pointing towards the house. Our cleaner walked towards the house and slowly pushed the front door open. I was sure he was bracing himself for whatever he might find on the other side.

"Gotttt damn!" We heard him yell out when he opened the front door. Two Spanish females followed behind him. The cleaning crew was here, so it was time for us to go.

19

"Stay right here. I'ma follow you home to make sure you good," Azul said to me before he followed Doley into the house.

I knew that he had to pay the cleaner and his crew for their services, so I made my way to the curb towards my parked white Lexus. My nerves were still bad. Seeing Azul lightly jog to his parked truck that was just across the street from me calmed my anxiety. He was my peace and had been since I was fourteen years old. When he got into his black-on-black Trackhawk Jeep and started the aggressive engine, I started my engine and led the way toward my apartment.

CHAPTER 2

AZUL

I swerved in and out of lanes driving behind Justice. Her ass drove just like me and it was because I was the one that taught her how to maneuver behind the wheel. I had taught her a lot in life and I bit my bottom lip in frustration just thinking of how those memories could have been the only thing I had left to hold on to. I cruised down her block in disbelief a bit. I was used to her hitting my trap phone for every little thing when it came to street business, but nothing like what I had walked in on. I was grateful that she was spared. The drive to her apartment was a quick one since she lived in Bedford Stuyvesant and the trap that had just been hit was in East New York.

When we got to her quiet tree-lined block, we both luckily found parks just right outside of her apartment building. I watched, as she exited her car. She was a ride-or-die for sure, and I needed her. Well, I had her; I just had to give her all of me. I was one meeting away from solidifying a new plug and, once I did, I was leaving Isabella's ass.

When I first met her, I told her my vision of becoming Brooklyn's King Pin and she put me in touch with her uncle. He liked me, but he said that the only way that he would sell to someone that wasn't full-bred Mexican was if they were married in. So, a nigga did what he had to. I had met Isabella in my senior year of high school when she transferred in. I knew that deep down, the relationship between her and I broke Justice to the core but, still, she stood by a nigga's side because she understood that all great things took sacrifice and that's what I was doing.

I thought that maybe with time, I would have gained some kind of feelings for Isabella romantically, but her spoiled, naïve mentality was a hard ass pill to swallow when I had a gangsta bitch like Justice at my side. She had a nice piece of pussy on her, but her gushy insides didn't grip me how Justice's did. I couldn't for the life of me understand how Justice was and had been so calm when it came to seeing the nigga she loved shack up with someone else. Had I been in that situation, I would kill any nigga that tried to approach her. I was territorial like that; what was mine was for me and no one else.

I looked out my tinted car window as I watched my first and only love waiting for me. Justice stood in front of her building with her hand placed on her small waist. Attitude. Little mama had so much attitude since we were kids and, with age, it only worsened. I knew that she was impatiently waiting for me to exit the vehicle, but I had to take her appearance in.

On a regular day like today, she sported a pair of ripped jeans that exposed that thigh tat of hers that I loved. A distressed Essentials shirt hugged those perky D-cups and a pair of blue Balenciagas I had gifted her for Valentine's Day dressed her cute chubby feet. She used her hand to push her loose hair up into the messy bun that she was wearing.

She knew that I loved it when she wore her hair out of her

face. It gave me a clear view to take in that nutmeg-colored

blemish-free skin tone. I exited my truck and hit the locks as

I walked in her direction.

"Thank you for making sure I made it home safe,"

she said as she took her house keys out of her purse. She

stood in front of the building's door in a way that sort of

blocked my path.

"I'm going to make sure you make it inside ya crib

safe too, so watch out," I said as I brushed past her, taking

my copy of keys out of my pocket in one swift move.

After holding the door open for her, she followed me

upstairs. The smell of clean linen invaded my nose as soon

as I opened her front door. Justice always kept a clean crib

for as long as I could remember. Hell, my trap houses were

spotless because of her. Making myself at home, I kicked off my sneakers as soon as I made it to her living room.

The bathroom was off to the side, so I headed that way. After turning on the water to the shower, I entered the living room and nodded my head toward the bathroom to signal for her to handle her hygiene. I knew that she had to wash the stale smell of horrible experience off of her. While she handled her business, I made my way to her tan suede sofa. Like I lived there, because I practically did, I grabbed the remote and channel surfed. *Power* faded as I slowly drifted into sleep...

"Mmmm," I grumbled.

Blinking my eyes slowly, it took me a while to fully wake. I looked down to find Justice wrapped in nothing but a towel with my tool in her mouth. "Sssss," I hissed as I grabbed the back of her head.

Her hair was damp, I guess from washing it. I looked at the sleeping screen of the smart television and saw that the time said 2:45 a.m. *Shit, Isabella is going to kill me,* I thought as I threw my head back and relaxed in the chair. Although there was never any romance in our relationship, I tried my hardest to make it home when I told her that I would. She never nagged a nigga about staying out, but she damn sure voiced her opinion when I didn't keep my word with her. Earlier that day, she simply asked if she should be expecting me home for the night, and I told her yes because I didn't have any intention of staying out.

I knew that I had to go, but Justice was making the battle so muthafucking hard for me. I let my eyes roll to the back of my head as I enjoyed the blow job that I was getting. Justice's head game skills were superb, and she knew it. It seemed like every time I came over, this was her way of getting me to stay.

"Ma, I can't stay," I whispered out in sort of a moan.

She took me out of her mouth like I was on fire or some shit. Smacking her juicy lips together, she kissed her teeth. It was obvious that I had pissed her off. She stood from the crouching position that she was just in and walked towards her bedroom. I watched her ass jiggle under the coral-colored towel as she swayed her hips.

"Love you, Ma!" I called out behind her.

She stuck her middle finger up to me in response and closed her room door behind her. Chuckling to myself, I put my soldier back into the slot of my underwear, zipped up my pants, put my sneakers back on, and made my way out. On the way down the stairs, I checked my cell phone to see that Doley had texted me.

Yo, I told Isabella that after the bar you crashed on my couch. You good for the night.

I smiled as I thought about going back inside Justice's apartment and staying the night. I decided against it because in the morning, I had a huge meeting at my office. In no time, I was home. Isabella was sound asleep in our bed, so I hopped in the shower really quickly and joined her.

***

Mornings in our three-bedroom penthouse were quiet as hell since we didn't have any children. The unit was a wedding gift from Isabella's uncle. It overlooked the Brooklyn bridge and, at night when the city line was lit up, it was a beautiful sight.

"Hey, you," Isabella cooed as she wrapped her arms around my waist.

She was far from an ugly girl. She resembled Eva Longoria in the face and in her body. I looked at our reflections in the mirror. On the surface, we made a damn good couple, but I knew better than that. Emotionally, we didn't connect with one another, and I hated forcing shit. Her high cheek bones rose with a smile. She puckered her lips, so I leaned down so that she could place a kiss on my cheek.

"You look good, Papa."

"Thanks, Mami."

I fixed the wrist on my dress shirt before grabbing the brush on the double sink to tame my waves. She tightened the silk robe that covered her slim frame before turning on her sink to brush her teeth. I watched her out of my peripheral vision. The silk material hugged that frame, and her little booty was poking. I eyed her with lust for a little moment because although my heart was with Justice, I was still a nigga at the end of the day. I shook my head from the nasty thoughts that I started to develop as I thought about the meeting I had scheduled in just a few hours.

Sitting down with Malik *Bleek* Browne was unheard of. He ran and operated The Ruiz Dynasty. Truth be told, I was just trying to get like him: a nigga headlining a Hispanic operation. He was the direct plug for a purer grade of coke straight from the Dominican Republic. I knew that he had his own little street crew running around in New York and up and down I-95.

I had no intention of stepping on their toes; I just wanted to eat beside them. No dick-riding shit, just thinking about the meeting had me geeked for real. It took me months to even line up a meet and, months before that, I had to sit down with myself to figure out a plan to even convince him to fuck with a nigga.

"What you got planned for the day?" I asked Isabella when she finished brushing her teeth.

"Just the gym and some shopping."

"The regular…" I was slightly disgusted, and I was sure my tone or my displeased facial expression showed it.

Besides shorty not being my soulmate, her day-to-day activities were a turn-off because this was all that she did. She had no substance to her life, and it was sickening for real. She raised her waxed arched eyebrow in my direction like she caught an attitude by my remark. I honestly didn't care enough to correct or apologize for what I had said.

"Mmm... enjoy your day," she said with much attitude as she slightly brushed past me on her way out of the bathroom, and I let her.

When we first got married, I used to handle her with kiddy gloves because I didn't want to lose my connect. Now, I didn't give a shit. To me, even if I didn't get Bleek as a new connect, I was prepared to have a sit down with Isabella's uncle to see if conducting business without me still being married to his niece was an option. We had created history and our own little bond from conducting business over the years, but I understood that family came first. If he wouldn't go for that, then I was even prepared to try and get a different connect from the Midwest. Either way, I was leaving

Isabella's ass. I had Justice on the back burner for too long, and enough was enough. More than anything, I was denying my own self-happiness just for a dime, and the shit was tiring.

I exited the bathroom and walked out of our room. I caught a glimpse of Isabella standing in her closet taking out some clothes for the day on my way out. I grabbed my suit jacket that was draped over the foot of the bed and put it on before grabbing my two phones and leaving out. My office was about fifteen minutes from the house, and I was thankful that the building had an underground parking garage because finding parking downtown was close to impossible. I hadn't been in the office for about two days and I was sure that there was a lot that needed my attention.

When I rolled into my first quarter of a million dollars, Justice convinced me to start any business that I could clean my money through. After trying to consider what would be the best option for me to go with, we started a private cleaning company. I had a team of cleaners that tended to homes, company buildings, and community centers. I also had a team of cleaners on the side that took care of all of my street messes.

"Hello Mr. Jones," my receptionist greeted me once I opened the glass doors that led to our suite.

"Good morning, Katie."

"I put your coffee on your desk next to some files, and I have a pot brewing in the break room for your ten o'clock meeting."

"Thank you."

I entered my office and closed the door behind me. Justice did her damn thing with hiring Katie. She was prompt and efficient. I checked the all-black Movado watch on my wrist and saw that I had about an hour until ten. I loosened my suit jacket and sat behind my French-imported desk. Another purchase that was all Justice's idea. The girl was hood as fuck, but she was classier than the prissy of prissy bitches. I pulled my phones from my slacks and placed both of them onto the wood surface. I grabbed one and then shot Justice a good morning text. I wanted her to feel special when she woke up this morning, and I knew that a simple *Good Morning Sexy Face* would do it.

After taking a couple of sips of my coffee, I tended to the files that were placed on my desk. The bulk of them were just invoices from the cleaning jobs over the past two weeks. Two other folders had inquiries from businesses that needed a quote with a service. Although I barely walked through the doors of this damn office, it ran effectively without me and a lot of that had to do with Justice. She visited this building way more than I did, and she made sure that everything ran efficiently in my absence. The bitch was a blessing for real.

When I got to the end of my coffee, I went into the break room to pour myself another cup. When I made it back to my office and took a seat, Katie peeked her head into the office.

"Mr. Jones, your ten o'clock is here. Mr. Browne, meet Mr. Jones."

Katie stood in the doorway of my office with just the man I needed to see standing behind her. She closed the door behind her, and I stood to shake hands with Malik.

"It's nice to finally meet you, Mr. Browne." I held my hand out.

He shook hands with me before sitting in one of the seats that stood on the other side of my desk.

"You can call me Bleek."

He sat back in the seat, and I quickly sat in mine. I wanted to get to business and get to it quickly. I didn't know if he was pressed for time, and I knew that I had one chance to try and lock this deal in. He sat across from me comfortable as a muthafucka. Most men sitting across from me seemed on edge but not him. You would have thought that my office belonged to his ass the way he seemed so carefree while sitting on the other side of the table from me.

My daddy used to tell me that the loudest one in the room was never the nigga with the money, and that's a code I lived by. I wasn't a fan of being flashy although, don't get me wrong, I did have a full closet of shit that would break the bank for some and, when I felt like it, muthafuckas could refer to me as Mr. Put That Shit On. Most of the time, I settled on the simple look because I didn't have shit to prove to any damn body. I could tell that the man seated across from me lived by my daddy's rule as well.

He wore a light pair of distressed denim jeans, a white t-shirt, and some gray New Balance 990 sneakers. His white gold Cuban linked chain was minimal but, being a man that loved jewelry, I knew that he had to drop a bag on that and his earrings. Walking past him on the street, one wouldn't have believed that he was a millionaire, let alone a King Pin.

Right when I was about to start talking, his phone started ringing. He leaned up in the chair and pulled his iPhone out of one of his pockets.

"I gotta take this," he said as his brows dipped while looking into his phone.

"Do ya thing."

"Hello? No, baby girl, you cannot wear your sister's shirt. Maylee, you can't even fit your sister's clothes. Listen, when I get back, I will take you to go and get the shirt in your size."

I sat back and watched, as he spoke into the phone. Instantly, I noticed his iced-out ring finger. That was what the fuck I wanted. The throne and the damn family to bring along for the ride.

"I will be back home tonight baby girl. Okay... love you most." He hung up his phone before turning his attention back to me. "Sorry about that. Family shit."

"I understand." And I did because badly, I couldn't wait to have all of that shit with Justice.

"So, have you cut ties with your Mexican connect? We have a history but nothing that should affect you leaving."

I didn't even know how he knew who was supplying me, but I should have known better. The hood told stories about the nigga sitting across from me.

"I would have had that done already, but it's kind of a sensitive situation because my wife is the connect's niece but I will have that handled by tomorrow."

"You gone stop doing business with the nigga but still be married to his niece?" He seemed confused and, honestly, the position that I was in was confusing as hell.

"Actually, I'm leaving my wife." That was my first time saying the shit out loud to anyone.

"Damn, well, it's life and shit happens but good; your shipment will be here by dawn. Of course, transportation fees will be added on," he said before he stood and started to exit. I was expecting to pitch myself before anything was set in stone. Not only had he agreed to supply me, but he had a shipment heading my way as we were speaking.

"So, that's it?" I asked as I stood from my seat. I wanted to walk him to the elevators.

"It is. I did my homework. Azul Jones, son of the late Zachariah and Zena Jones. You only started selling dope to pay for your mother's surgery to remove her cancer after ya pops passed. That's admirable as fuck by the way. The number one rule in this game is to take care of the fam and to take care of the niggas that take care of you. That's how you keep the team loyal. I'm pretty sure after seeing all of that money, you just couldn't stop though, huh? You stand ten toes and have since hitting the scene, what was it? Nine years ago?" He paused and, when I nodded my head that he was correct, he finished speaking, "I don't meet with just anyone and I damn sure don't meet with anybody that I don't have intentions of doing business with. I like ya style because you keep ya crew small and stay discreet; this shell business is a prime example of that. My right-hand man, Sha, will be in touch with your shipment. You can send my payment to the offshore account that he will give you."

I couldn't help but let a small smile creep onto my face.

"Yeah, it's okay to smile nigga. You're about to see the most money you've ever seen in your life," he said.

I let my firm exterior break when the corners of my mouth turned upward.

"There we go," Bleek laughed before slapping fives with me.

"Let me walk you out, man." I held the door open for him, and we made our way toward the elevators.

"Do you have a loading dock here?" he asked.

"We do, it's in the back."

"Aight cool, ya shipment can be dropped here or you can choose another location. I have three auto shops out here if you want to pick up ya shit from there. It's up to you. Let Sha know what you are rolling with, and he'll inform me."

"Umm… I don't have a contact for Sha."

"He'll contact you."

"Got it."

The elevator doors opened, and I slapped fives with him. Before he stepped inside, his phone rang again and, this time, he quickly answered it.

"Yes, Mrs. Browne, I'm good. I'm leaving now. Yes, I told Maylee that I will take her shopping when I get back. So, now Maliah and MJ want to go shopping too? Greatttttt," he dragged.

He gave me a head nod before the doors closed. I laughed to myself because as badly as I wanted the family man lifestyle, I wasn't quite ready to deal with the children part of it. I was only twenty-seven years old, and my main focus was stacking my bread.

When I got back to the privacy of my office, I did a little two-step because a nigga was excited as fuck. Not only was I about to have the purest shit flooding the streets but I had got in good with the most elite of the elite. I snatched one of my phones off my desk and noticed that Justice hadn't texted me back yet. I saw that Isabella had shot me a text but I didn't even have the decency to open it. Fuck whatever had to be handled at the office today, I was going straight to Justice's crib to share this amazing news.

For months, I had been keeping all of this shit from her and, finally, it felt good to be able to breathe a little. I never kept shit from Justice, so I found myself biting the insides of my cheeks when around her just to keep this shit from her, and it was killing me. She was finally going to know that one, I had locked down a better connect than what we had and, two, I was leaving Isabella.

CHAPTER 3

ISABELLA

I hated the feeling I had in the pit of my gut when Azul closed the door behind him. I felt sick to my stomach and I was sure it was because I hadn't eaten yet for the morning. I lied and told him that I had a day planned of going to the gym and then shopping but, in all actuality, I had something special planned for him. I could feel my husband slipping through my fingers, and that was the last thing that I wanted. A candlelit dinner sounded like the start of a remedy to me.

I quickly threw on a sweatsuit with some running shoes. When my stomach growled, I knew that Starbucks was calling my name. I grabbed my LV monogram purse and my car keys and headed out the door. As I waited in line to order my breakfast, I thought about the disgust Azul had in his tone when he asked me what I had planned for the day.

44

When he met me, he knew that I was spoiled. My uncle made sure of it, and it was clear that by being with me he had to take that torch and run with it. By marrying me, he knew that he had to keep up with the lifestyle that I was accustomed to. Tio made sure to supply him with the financial stability to keep up with my needs.

"Mam, are you ready?"

I didn't even notice that I was holding up the line being stuck in my thoughts.

"Yes... can I have a spinach, feta, and egg white wrap and a... venti caramel frap... wait," I thought how my doctor just told me a couple of days ago that I should cut back on the caffeine, "make that a tall."

"Yes, sure!"

I gave the girl my name and stood off to the side while I waited for my order. Before leaving the house, I had noticed that Azul was running low on his favorite cologne, so I made a mental note to stop into Neiman Marcus to get him another bottle. I got my order and took a seat nearby so that I could enjoy it. Scrolling through my phone, I sent Azul a message wishing he would enjoy the rest of his day. When he left as early as he did and in a suit, I knew that I probably wouldn't see him until later in the night. That gave me more than enough time to get to the house and situate it how I wanted to.

I saw that my uncle had called me twice the day prior. Knowing that he didn't function properly until the afternoon, I told myself that I would call him back later. For the life of me, I couldn't shake what Azul had said about how I spend my days. We were nine years into our marriage and, for the entire nine, my days consisted of shopping, working out, or redecorating a room in the house. I knew that soon, my day-to-day would change, but I wanted to make an effort to add something productive before that happened.

In high school, I used to love doing hair. I would give all of the girls wash and sets, not for money but just for fun. I had *growing hands*, as some of them used to say. I couldn't see myself in the near future standing on my feet for prolonged times, but I did have a love for doing hair.

I grabbed my iPad out of my purse and jotted down a list of things that I should start working on to get a salon open. I wanted to be hands-on with my business so, instead of reaching out to my uncle for him to point me in the right direction, I wanted to take control and get the shit done myself. This would be more great news that I could share over dinner later with Azul.

With marrying him, I knew that a lot of his reason for it was to get to my uncle, and I understood that. Back in high school, he was sweet and genuine as hell. He didn't walk on eggshells around me how everyone else did just because of who I was. That alone attracted me to him, he was his own person; and it didn't matter who an individual was or what they did, it never swayed him away from being authentic.

After eating, I got myself together to leave Starbucks. I had a long list of things to do and I better had started with my task.

***

"Tío, something is wrong."

I held my iPhone to my ear with my shoulder as I spoke on the phone with my uncle. Whenever I needed advice on anything, I went to him. He was a listening ear, and his mouth was filled with wisdom. My uncle was more like my dad than anything. My father was shot and killed back in Mexico in a drive-by shooting when I was ten years old. So, happily, Tío Alejandro stepped up and walked in my father's shoes because he had no children of his own.

When I was sixteen years old, he picked up and moved us to Brooklyn. Wanting to shelter and protect me, he had me homeschooled for my junior year. I couldn't take much more of that shit, so I rebelled until he finally agreed to let me attend public school for my senior year. That's when I met Azul and the rest was honestly history.

Earlier in the day after finishing my errands, my very last task ended five minutes from Azul's job. Wanting to surprise him, I picked up some lunch to take to his office. When I got there, his receptionist informed me that he had left for the day. Not understanding why he hadn't responded to my morning text without being drowned in work frustrated me, so I called him, only for both of his phones to go straight to voicemail. I stayed far away from his street life because honestly, I wanted nothing to do with it.

Growing up, my uncle told me how he made his own income, but he sheltered me for the most part. Azul moved the same way because I knew that he knew that I wasn't the ride-until-the-wheels-fell-off kind of girl. As soon as the check engine light came on, I was tucking and rolling out of the car. With knowing that, still, Azul would shoot me a text if he was maneuvering out in the streets.

As I stood in front of his receptionist, I eagerly searched my phone for a message from him letting me know that he was 'handling business', as he would call it. That nagging gut feeling of infidelities occurring crept into the depths of my soul. I was not stupid and, over the years, he had come in late or sometimes not even at all, but I never had the want to ask if he was ever cheating on me. In my head, I wanted to believe that my marriage was perfect.

My uncle broke me from my thoughts.

"What is wrong my love?"

It was like as soon as someone asked what's wrong, the floodgates threaten to open. I sniffled to keep that at bay before I responded, "I think Azul is going to leave me."

I didn't want to reveal my suspicion of cheating until I had some hardcore facts. My uncle took marriage very seriously. He had been married to my Tia all my life, and I never once saw him disrespect her. Besides being about his money, he was about his family.

"Now, why would he do such a thing when his business is going so well?"

"I don't know Tío, but I can feel it." The tormenting feeling was crippling me.

"*Sobrina*, I'm sure he wouldn't leave you while you're with child. This must be the hormones talking. *Tomalo con calma bene*."

His strong heavy Spanish accent put me at ease. I didn't see how he could expect me to take it easy when I felt my husband slipping through my fingers. Azul didn't know about my pregnancy, but I spent all morning getting decorations for our dining room so that I could break the news to him over dinner. If our love couldn't grow and blossom on its own, then I was sure that our baby could bring us together. I played with the wedding ring on my finger as I listened to my uncle's words of encouragement. To make me feel better, he ended the conversation with the threat of breaking Azul's legs if he ever left me.

After getting off the phone with him, I ran myself a bath because I needed to relax my mind and body. I looked at my slim naked frame in the mirror and tried to envision what a pregnant belly would look like on me. I turned to the side and placed my palm right at my waist. I tilted my head to the side and squinted to see if I could see a baby tummy on me, but I couldn't. I grabbed my hair and put it into a loose top knot.

The water was finally to my liking, so I slid my body into the marble tub. I sighed deeply as I rested my back on the back of the tub. I tried to envision what our house would be like with the sound of a baby crying or the sound of the little pitter-patter of a toddler's feet. My life was about to change drastically, and I needed to tighten up and get my head together so that I could be the best me for my child.

***

JUSTICE

I squinted my eyes as the sun's rays peeked through the blinds of my bedroom. I would have had my blackout curtains pulled shut if I had partaken in my nightly routine. After Azul left, I grabbed a personal bottle of Hennessy off my bar and took it to the face. My head was pounding as I rolled over and tossed the cover over my shoulder. When I couldn't find my comfortable spot, I snatched the blanket off my frame and walked towards my bathroom. I needed to get my mind right. I knew that a shower would relieve some of the hangover symptoms that I was experiencing. I ran my water and waited for it to warm up. I never walked around the house in clothes, that's why I was thankful that I made enough money to live on my own.

I wasn't close to my sister, but I knew her bum ass was living with her no-good-ass ex just so that she could get her bills paid. Being a single mother was a struggle that she was losing horribly. She couldn't pay bills on her own and the inflation in the United States didn't make it any better. That's one thing about living in New York; you had muthafuckas broken up but still living together because the price of rent was so damn high.

Once the water was warm enough to my liking, I jumped in. I gathered water into the palms of my hands and splashed it onto my face. If this hot ass shower didn't work, I knew that I would feel better after some breakfast. I filled my hands with water again. As I wiped the sleep out of my eyes, I heard my front door opening. One thing about me was that my spidey senses were always on high.

I quietly pulled my shower curtain back just enough to stick my head out. When I heard footsteps coming my way, I looked at the sink's counter and realized that I didn't bring my phone into the bathroom with me. It was too early in the morning for it to be Azul. With all of the bullshit going on with Trav, I was mad at myself for being comfortable enough to not bring my gun into the bathroom with me. It was a damn shame that I couldn't even feel relaxed in my own home. My worst fear was being shot with my own damn gun.

I closed the shower curtain when I saw the knob to the door turning. When the door opened, I grabbed my loofa and stood still. I got slightly lightheaded from holding my breath. I was mad as fuck that I had gotten a thick ass shower curtain because I couldn't see what whoever was doing. I heard the toilet seat lift and what sounded like somebody pissing in my toilet. I snatched the curtain back fast as hell, and there was a loud noise from the curtain hooks gliding across the rod.

Azul pissed on my floor as he turned around quickly. He was about to reach for his gun, but he made eye contact with me. "Fuck you doing scaring a nigga?"

He shook off before sliding his tool back into his slacks. I waited for the noise from the toilet flushing to finish before I responded.

"Scaring you? You scared my ass coming over unannounced."

When he finished cleaning up my floor, he offered me a response, "A nigga don't need to announce his presence when he has a key."

I had this thing for letting the shower water run for a while before I even entered the bathroom, so I was sure that he didn't think that I was behind the curtain. When he started undressing, I raised my eyebrow.

"What the hell you think you doing? If you stopped by to use the bathroom, that's cool. You did that, now, you can leave. Although you should have just pissed outside like the dog you are."

"Man, cut it the fuck out. I got great news and I need some celebratory nani."

"You not getting a damn thing!"

I slid the curtain closed and continued to wash my body. My nipples hardened from the slight breeze when Azul opened the curtain before entering the shower behind me.

"I'm not getting what?"

He stood behind me and, being that I was only 5'5, his thick pole sat on top of my lower back. He pushed up against me and, instantly, my garden was wet with anticipation of him entering.

"I'm not getting what?" he asked again, this time followed by a kiss on my neck.

"Zoo I'm dead ass seriou—"

I couldn't even finish my statement when he pushed me up against my white subway tiles and crouched down so that he could enter me. I gasped at his girth.

I had been taking that thick ass rod since I was eighteen. Somewhere amid our friendship, I had cracked the door open to the friend zone and his ass used his foot and kicked that shit in.

"Mmmm." I arched my back as he dug out my middle.

"What you said I wasn't getting now?" he asked before gently nibbling on my ear.

"You wasn't getting this."

"What's this?"

Smack!

He slapped my ass as he rotated his hips in a circular motion to hit my spot.

"This pussy," I moaned out.

"Who pussy?"

The sounds of my gushy insides sounded over the sound of the water coming from the shower head.

"Who…" *smack* "pussy" *smack* "is this?"

"YOURS," I cried out as my honey coated his shaft.

"You gone cum again for me?"

I placed my hands on the tiles to give myself enough leverage to throw it back.

"Shit…" he hissed under his breath.

"You gone cum for me?" I talked my shit.

He was a pleaser when it came to sex, so he always made sure I got mine before he got off. He grabbed me by the hips and started pounding my insides.

"You want me to cum Ma?"

If I would have had my nails done, I was sure I would have broken one, the way I was gripping the tiles.

"Yesss Pa."

"Ssssss, you love me?"

I hated when he got too deep into the love shit when we were fucking. I loved the shit out of Azul Jones; I just hated that I shared him. Instantly, tears filled my eyes.

"Justice? You love ya nigga?"

With every thrust, he dug a little deeper into my middle and, with every stroke, I inched closer to yet another climax.

"Hmmm," I moaned.

"Answer me, Ma; you love ya nigga?"

"Yes Pa, I love you."

"I'm cummin," he whispered all out of breath.

When I felt him throbbing in my insides, I came right along with him. He pressed his body against mine as we both breathed deeply. We didn't partake in many quickies but, when we did, whew; the shit was Grade-A sex for sure.

"I love you, Justice," he said as he kissed my cheek before pulling out.

I couldn't stand when he would spill his seeds into me because I wasn't ready for a child; I wouldn't even know what to do with one. Luckily, God had been keeping a watchful eye over me because whenever my next period was due after his shenanigans, I would send a silent prayer. He grabbed my rag that hung in the shower, handed it to me, and then grabbed his own. The shower we took was a silent one. I was pretty sure that he had a lot on his mind.

Whenever he went quiet, I couldn't read him, and I hated that for me. When we were finished, he cut the water off and stepped out of the shower. When those big ass size thirteen feet slapped across my tiled floor, I cringed. I hated that he didn't dry his feet off first before stepping out of the shower. Little things like that were what made me appreciate living alone as well. When he handed me my towel, I smiled before taking it from him. He walked out of the bathroom with his body still wet and dick swinging.

"Why my towel wasn't hanging behind the door?" he asked with a raised eyebrow as he dried his body off with a new towel he had gotten from my linen closet.

"I had to do laundry."

"But the rags were still in the shower?"

"Azul, I fucking forgot about them; what's the problem?"

This muthafucka had some damn nerve. A whole married nigga pressing me about something in my damn house.

"If you had a nigga over, speak up."

And there it was, he knew how to fuck up a good time. I quickly dried my feet, stepped out of the shower, wrapped the towel tightly around my body, and tucked the fabric under my arms.

"I think it's best you go back home to your wife." I pushed pass him and made my way toward my bedroom. His voice followed behind me.

"So, you ain't gone say it."

"Say the fuck what!" I raised my voice when I didn't mean to, but this nigga had me fucked up. "You got a key to this bitch. Fuck I look like having a nigga walking around this muthafucka. You have a whole damn wife and you on my back abou—"

"I'm leaving her tonight."

I stopped speaking and just stared at him for a bit. He never said that shit out of his mouth to me. I cared about

Azul, I did but, more than anything, I cared about my livelihood and getting to my bag.

"And what about the connect?"

That was his main reason for even marrying Isabella and his marriage was what kept food in the crew's mouths. Call me crazy, but he would have to stay married to that prissy bitch if it meant that I lived to eat another day.

"I found a new one."

"How did you manage?"

"Come on Ma, I had this in the works for a while."

I couldn't help the smile from spreading across my face. He was really doing this shit. I was already getting the money and, now, I was going to get the nigga too. After drying off fully, I grabbed one of his t-shirts out of his drawer and pulled it over my head to put on.

"Hand me a pair of drawers."

I tossed him a pair of his boxers before getting in my bed.

"We ordering food in?" he asked as he laid next to me.

"Yeah, that's cool."

He grabbed my phone that sat on top of the comforter and went to the Door Dash app to order us some breakfast. Knowing me inside and out, he ordered my favorite from our favorite restaurant. My mouth watered just thinking about the home fries, sunny-side-up eggs, sausage, and toast.

I laid in my comfort zone. The spot under his armpit was made just for me. With one ear, I listened to his heartbeat while with the other, I listened to the show that he was watching on television. I was still drained from the night before honestly so, I was sure that after I ate, I would go back to sleep.

"Ma, I do need you to do something though."

"What's that?" I asked before letting out a long yawn.

"I need you at my side when our first shipment gets dropped off. Like, this is really an accomplishment for me, for us."

"Of course, I wouldn't have it any other way. When does the shipment get dropped off?"

"By tonight."

I lifted my head from his chest and stared him in his eyes. He was moving quickly as hell. He put my head back onto his chest before continuing, "Well, tomorrow damned near. The load is scheduled to be at the loading dock by five in the morning."

"Will Doley be there too?" This was an accomplishment for all three of us, and I wanted to make sure that my bro wasn't left out.

"Na, he has other shit to take care of. I'll make sure we have some guys for extra protection just in case."

"Na, that's not even needed." I wasn't feeling anybody being present for my protection because in my eyes, if he was there, that's all I needed and, besides, Azul's protection couldn't nobody protect me better than me.

"We'll at least need two people to help us offload shipment Ma."

"Then do that," I said before yawning again.

Azul and I spent the rest of the day wrapped in each other. It was nice for a change to be in each other's presence without the distraction of phones. The quality time definitely gave me a sneak peek into what life would be like with him every day. Breakfast lunch and dinner were ordered in and, in between meals, we took each other's bodies on highs that we hadn't before.

I was open as fuck and hours after the sunset and the smell of barbecue crept into my window from my neighbor's cooking out, I dozed off with him lying beside me. I knew that he had business to handle so, when my 4 am alarm went off, I knew that he wouldn't be lying beside me. He had to go handle his scandal with Isabella, but I was hopeful that he would have all of that shit squared away before our shipment touched down.

CHAPTER 4

DOLEY

"David, I want to go on a vacation."

I sat back on my sofa as I listened to my girl, Imon, complain all morning. She was spoiled as hell, and I didn't have anyone to blame but my damn self because this was what I had turned her into. Imon had been down with me since my first year in college. I did two years at a local community college, just so that I could be more knowledgeable in the business management field. When I realized just how many students gliding across campus were off that nose candy, I knew that I would make a fortune there. Within two years, I had built a nice chunk of people that were coming straight to me to cop.

After graduating, I mainly helped Zoo with his business ventures because I hadn't decided which business I wanted to embark on for myself.

69

"Hellooooo," Imon was snapping her pretty manicured fingers in my face, "I want to vacation."

I looked around her because she was standing in front of the television. When she placed her hand on her small waist and shifted all of those 175 pounds to one leg, I knew that she had a big-ass attitude. I opened the armrest to the recliner chair that I was sitting in and gave her four stacks of money.

"Go vacation then."

She rolled her eyes all while snatching the money out of my hand. "I want you to go with me," she begged.

"Can't."

I was detached from my emotions and always had been. Everyone around me knew it. I had love for her but I just refused to show that shit. I loved my mother to death at one point in time, and she was the first woman to break my heart. After that shit, no woman couldn't get that close to me.

Imon made it this far because she was willing to deal with my lack of affection and mood swings from time to time. I was sure the money was helping her cope with my bullshit. Bitches put aside a lot of shit and healed from heartbreak faster than Wolverine when a nigga got that bag, and I indeed had the bag. It didn't matter that she had her own money; it was always nice for a nigga to be able to financially take care of things and I could do that plus more.

"I'm thinking Miami," she said out loud.

"Do it." I looked around her to make it known that I was trying to catch the college basketball highlights.

She sucked her teeth before finally moving out of my way. After hearing my room door slam, I was sure that she was packing the little bit of things that she had at my house. She always went through the dramatic shit when I would rub her the wrong way. I only gave her a drawer to put her things in at my crib, although I had his and her closets. I didn't even allow her to stay more than thirty days at a time. I didn't need anyone trying to establish residency in my shit. When she stormed past me with her Gucci backpack swung over her shoulder, I watched as her ass jiggled in her bicycle shorts.

"Let me know when you get home." I cared about her short chocolate ass.

"Fuck you, David."

I laughed once she slammed my front door. I sat on the edge of the recliner as I focused back on the television. "There he goes," I mumbled to myself.

I had to hand it to Trav's little brother, Tremaine, he was skilled on the court. It was truly unfortunate that I had to take a trip to Buffalo State to go and snatch his ass up. Zoo was busy solidifying another plug for us, so it was time for me to get my hands dirty. Trav had to have been crazy to rob us, and it was clear that he lost his fucking mind for killing two of our workers. Getting at him was like getting at us, close to impossible. That's when I remembered that he had a little brother that used to play street ball.

After putting my ear to the streets, in no time, I was able to find him. I wasn't looking forward to the damn near seven-hour drive, but it had to be done. I tossed some clothes into one of my duffle bags just in case I needed to stay a couple of days. The school had a home game that night and, after what I was sure would be a win for Buffalo State, I was going to snatch up their star player.

***

Anything outside of the city had me on edge for real. The summer's weather felt amazing in Brooklyn but, upstate, it had a little chill that made me zip my Nike Tech hoodie all the way up to my damn chin. One thing I loved about colleges was the food places around them bitches. I was stuffing some cheese fries into my mouth as I tried to find parking on the visitor's lot. By the time I walked in, the game was damn near done, so I stood on the sideline and blended in with the large crowd of people just standing around.

The sound of muthafucking sneakers was starting to irk the fuck out of me. More than that, the gym was filled with college students' cheers and rants. The score was close and, I had to give it to Tremaine, he was locked in and in beast mode. Watching him on a screen was one thing, but seeing that little nigga work the court in person was different. I looked at the scoreboard as the bright red numbers counted down drastically.

7...6...5...4...3...2...

Swish!

It was like everyone in the gym heard the ball glide into the hoop and, as soon as it did, everybody started cheering. That cocky muthafucka started doing this little hip dance, and the rest of the niggas on the team started that bullshit. I had an old soul, so all that gyrating wasn't my bop. The next thing I knew, everyone around me was rocking their fucking hips.

"Hell muthafucking no," I mumbled.

I pushed my way out of the celebrating crowd to exit for the car. I sat and waited for a little minute. I knew that, more than likely, the basketball team would have gone out to celebrate. I sat in a rental and rolled me one up while I impatiently waited.

The ball players exited the gym and all got into different cars. My main focus was following behind Tremaine so, when he hopped into a powder blue Charger, I discreetly followed behind. It was obvious that his brother spoiled him or that he had his own little motion to get him in a car like that.

The lot outside of the nightclub was packed. After parking, I kept close to the group when I saw that the bouncer was letting members of the basketball team in. My attire of a sweatsuit had me blending in with the college kids. Well, that and my baby face. I had shaved down my scruffy beard before taking that long drive so that I could blend in with the kiddos. I knew that I was a certified old man when the bass from the music started giving me a migraine.

I saw that Tremaine and this little crew were tucked away in one of the back sections. I took a mental note of what he was dressed in before I retreated back to the car. Those little niggas were living on top of the world. Young city girls were thirsty as hell off their young lit asses. I brushed past a gang of them as I made my exit. Once I sat comfortably in the rental, I reclined the seat back a bit. Rolling my weed kept me level-headed, especially on a drill. I hated that I needed a controlled substance to handle business, but it had been that way since high school.

While I waited on my target, I scrolled on my Instagram account. I only had one hundred followers and I was sure most of them were bots. I kept a low profile, and the only reason why I had an account, to begin with was because Imon was big on that shit. The first story bubble that I saw illuminated in green was from her.

When I clicked her story, I saw that she was shaking her ass on the beach. She must have made it safely to Miami and she couldn't even let a nigga know. I thumbed up her story and then moved on to the next one. Zoo posted on his story, *Damn*, with the emoji of the nigga covering his face. I didn't know what that was about, but I was sure that I would get filled in over a bottle of Henny later when I hit the town. I busied myself with some games of Uno on my phone while I waited for Tremaine to make his exit.

Throughout the night, members of the basketball team started to trickle out of the club. These new niggas didn't move how me and my niggas would have moved. On the handful of times growing up that Zoo, me, and the rest of the gang hit the scene, we all rolled together. We pulled up in a spot together and, when it was time to go, we all left together as a unit.

"We got action," I whispered to myself when I saw Tremaine exit with some big booty bitch.

Where he parked his car, he had to cross right in front of mine, and I loved that for me. I quickly twisted the silencer on the end of my snub and pulled my ski mask over my face. I pressed the button to pop the trunk and, quietly, I exited the car and followed behind them. I didn't want to have to do it to the bitch but I didn't have time for her screaming.

WHACK!

The sound of the metal hitting the back of her head hopefully sounded way worse than it was. The impact of the hit I knew would knock her ass right on out. She fell to the floor quickly and, when she did, Tremaine turned around.

"Ahhh shit... come on now bro, like I ain't even nobody."

"Shut the fuck up little nigga," I said through gritted teeth.

I grabbed him up and walked with him to the trunk of the car. The little nigga didn't even try to fight back, and that's when I knew he had no street in his ass. His fight or flight mode must have been broken because he didn't even try to make a run for it either. One thing I drilled into myself in this life was that a nigga would have to kill me where I stood because there was no way in hell I was letting anyone take me anywhere.

"Open the trunk little nigga," I said lowly.

"Ahhh, come on bro. I got this thing with tight spaces. I'm homophobic."

I started laughing because I was sure that he didn't have any fucking smarts. His skills on the court were what his little dumb ass was riding on for sure. I pushed the gun into his rib cage, and his ass opened that trunk fast as fuck.

"Nigga, it's claustrophobic and don't worry about tight spaces; you gone be sleep."

"Huh?"

Before his ass could say anything else, I whacked him with the nose to the gun and pushed his ass into the trunk. I grabbed the duct tape that was beside him, wrapped him at the ankles and wrist, and tossed a couple of pieces over his mouth for good measure. I had a long ass drive to do and I knew that I had to stop somewhere in between to make sure that the little nigga was still breathing. I grabbed the tape and scissors and closed the trunk.

If it were up to me, I would have bodied the little nigga in the parking lot, but Zoo wanted him captured and brought the fuck in. He said that he wanted to send a message and, if you asked me, a dead body was the best message but I guess he had other plans for the little nigga.

I hopped into the driver's seat and grabbed my burner phone out of the glove compartment. Zoo didn't text me, and I told him that I wouldn't hit his ass until I made it to one of our warehouses with this nigga. Being that I didn't know what he had planned, I made a mental note to give him a heads-up of my return when I was a bit closer to Brooklyn.

As I pulled out of the lot and drove pass the club, I saw that three of the basketball players were looking around as they exited. I was sure that they were looking for Tremaine's ass. I laughed a bit because I already knew that they wouldn't see his ass ever again. I turned up the radio and tried to do the dash on the way back to Brooklyn.

CHAPTER 5

AZUL

With an empty sack and a clear mind, I was prepared to break things off with Isabella. I had already texted Alejandro that we needed to meet. I was a man that stood ten toes, and me replacing him as my plug was a conversation that needed to be done in person. I stood at the door with my keys in my hand for a while. I was a little nervous, so I zipped down the sweater to my sweatsuit. I was more comfortable in the attire that dressed me. I had ditched the suit before leaving Justice's place. I had so many clothes at her crib that I considered upsizing her a few years ago, but she was comfortable where she was. She grew up in Bedford-Stuyvesant and, although she wasn't close to her sister or her mother, she wanted to be nearby just in case they ever needed her for anything. Her heart was big like that.

Her living in an apartment was cool when it was just her. After dissolving all ties with Isabella and the business dealings I had with her uncle, it was time for me and Justice to upsize to a house. Queens or Long Island seemed like a good fit for us. I fumbled with my keys at the front door because there was a lot on my mind. I didn't know how Isabella would take it when I broke the news to her. For the most part, she was a chill soul, but I knew that there was always a pit of fire lying dormant within those Spanish bitches.

As soon as I opened the door, the smell of seafood filled my nostrils. I was already full from the Dallas BBQs that Justice and I had for dinner. When I saw gold balloons floating in the air and saw that the lights were dimmed, I sucked my teeth. Out of all days of her wanting to do some spontaneous shit, why did it have to be on the night when I had all intent on ending things?

"Isabella!" I called out.

Light R&B music played throughout the house. Quickly, I walked around trying to find her. My travels ended in our dining room. The table held a seafood spread; she knew that shit was my favorite.

"Why are you yelling Papi?"

I checked my watch to make sure that it wasn't a nigga's birthday or some shit. More gold balloons filled the room we stood in. "What's all of this?" I asked.

On the floor in the corner was a shit load of designer gift bags. Her smile was bright and beautiful. She had this glow on her face like she was the happiest woman in the world. When I left the house that morning, she didn't seem too pleased with me, so I wondered what had her this thrilled.

"I just think that we need a special night to ourselves you know."

She grabbed the bottle of champagne that was sitting on ice and popped the cork. I moved to the side quickly so that the shit didn't hit me.

"Here my love." She handed me a halfway-filled champagne glass.

She opened a bottle of apple juice and poured it into another flute for herself. My mental rolodex started churning rapidly. She had been sick last week and told me it was some bad sushi she had, her face was fucking glowing and, now, she wasn't drinking with me.

"Nigga, you pregnant?" I couldn't help myself from blurting out.

There was a happy glimmer in her eyes that pissed me off. She didn't even have to answer me verbally. The smile that spread across her face gave me the answer that I needed. When I stared at her for too long with a straight face, her smile faded.

"Is there a problem with your *wife* being pregnant?"

The heavy emphasis she put on the word wife and the way her arched eyebrow was raised made me screw my face up. Being real was going to hurt her, but I had to snatch that band-aid off quickly. This wasn't the time for me to coddle her ass if I wanted to make a clean break.

"Isabella, cut the shit. It's been a while since I've treated you like my *wife*."

Before I could finish my statement, she grabbed a circular plate from off the table and hurled it in my direction. I dodged the hit but I definitely felt the wind it created as it glided past my head.

"Bitch, you crazy?" I barked.

"Estoy loca!?"

She picked up another plate and hurled it in my direction again.

"Yes, bitch, are you crazy!?" I yelled as I dodged another flying damn saucer.

Over the years, I learned to fluently speak and understand Spanish. There was no way I was going to conduct business with a nigga or lie with a bitch without knowing it when it was their first language.

"Azul, I am your wife…"

When she started to cry, honestly, I did start to feel a bit bad. I just expected her to know what shit was from the jump and to follow with it. I didn't take into account that while for nine years, I always had Justice at my side, she had nobody. To be honest, I didn't think I would have cared if she did get her a little side piece, but she wasn't like that. She wasn't a street bitch but she was a loyal girl when committed. Overall, she was a good woman, shit, a great one. She just wasn't the woman for me.

When the whimpers escaped her body, I closed the space between us and wrapped my arms around her.

"This baby can make us better," she cried into my chest.

"It can't but you know that."

I rubbed her back as I let her get her emotions out. Badly, I wanted to ask her for an abortion, but that wouldn't be fair of me. This wasn't nobody's fault but mine. For years, I had always taken the precaution to prevent pregnancy in my marriage but, as of late, I had slacked on it. It would be childish shit like Justice getting on my nerves over something small; then, I would come home and fuck the shit out of Isabella, most likely drunk off a bottle of Tequila.

We stood in the dining room for what felt like forever. The smell of the shrimp on the table was calling my name, so I reached my arm out and snatched one off the table and ate it all while still consoling her.

"Are you eating at a time like this?" she asked with a sniffle.

Quickly, I chewed the shrimp that was in my mouth and tossed the shell back onto the table. "Mmm mmmm," I said as I quickly chewed the shrimp in my mouth.

"You really don't give a shit about anything."

She pushed me out of the way and exited the room. I grabbed two more shrimps and ate them before following behind her.

"Isabella?" I called out.

When I entered our room, she was sitting on our bed. The bandage dress she wore was sexy and burgundy in color. She had her long hair in loose curls and her makeup was lightly done. She wore a burgundy lip, and she knew I loved that shit. Something about the way she would leave a burgundy ring around my dick when she gave me head wearing that shade of lipstick did it for me every time. She had put so much into making the night special, and I had to ruin it.

I sighed deeply before taking a seat on the bench that stood at the foot of our bed. She was having trouble with the clasp to her heel, so I reached over and took them off for her.

"Is there someone else?" she finally mustered up the courage to ask.

In nine years, she had never asked me this question. I spent nights coming in late or not even coming home at all, and she never bothered to ask if there was someone else. Some women just lived their lives wanting to be wives or mothers, and that's the energy that Isabella gave. If having those things were at the top of her priority list, then I knew for damn sure that she was keeping this baby and I just knew that this divorce was about to be hell.

"Azul..."

I blinked before looking in her direction. Her brown eyes were pleading with me and the tip of her pointed nose was red in color from her crying.

"Is there someone else?" she asked again.

"Yeah." I'd let her ass get me for alimony later for the infidelities because I couldn't lie anymore.

"Hijo de puta!!" she yelled as she stood from the bed and knocked everything off her nightstand.

She was right; I was a *son of a bitch* for not coming clean years ago. I took off the hoodie to my sweatsuit because I knew that it was going to be a long night ahead of me. She tore our bedroom up, and I let her. She needed to get all of those emotions out, and I wasn't about to stop shit because stopping her could lead to her hitting me.

One thing about me, my mother had always taught me to be a man and keep my hands to myself but, if a bitch swung, I would be more than happy to knock her ass out. I felt like if I practiced keeping my hands to myself, then they should too. I remember Justice bucked up one day a couple of years back and punched me dead in my face. I slapped the shit out of her so hard that I was sure the taste buds on the right side of her tongue still didn't work till this day.

Crash... boom...

She was in my closet going to work. I already knew that my mirrors were broken and my glass sneaker display was in shambles. I leaned up from my seat when one of my phones vibrated.

Doley: Almost to the spot with this load. Meet me at the spot tomorrow?

Right when I was about to respond to him, Isabella snatched the phone out of my hand and threw it at the wall. I already knew that my screen had to have shattered because she threw that shit like she was trying to make it into the major leagues.

"Fuck is ya problem?" I was fed the fuck up with this tantrum she was having.

"It's that ghetto bitch *Justice*. Isn't it?" She was seething and obviously furious because spit was flying out of her mouth as she yelled in my face.

I wiped the flying specs off my face with the back of my hand. "Watch your mouth when talking about her…"

SLAP!

"Fuck you! You're a piece of shit!" she screamed in my face, as I ran my tongue across the front row of my teeth.

When I tasted blood, I stood from my seat. I hovered over her small stature. I wanted to slap the fuck out of her, but she was a crying mess. "Keep your hands to yourself," I lowly said as I tried to walk pass her.

She grabbed the back of my shirt. "Azul, please! We can be a family!" She was screaming so loud and crying that

I just knew the neighbors would call the damn police. "Pleaseeeee," she begged.

This sour patch head ass bitch was irking me for real. She was flipping back and forth between being angry and wanting things to work. Bitch had to be pregnant because those hormones were all over the place. I turned around and gently removed her clasped hands from my t-shirt. She was stretching my shit out.

"How far are you?" I asked, and that seemed to calm her. I needed all of my information before bringing this to Justice.

"Thirteen weeks."

Quickly, I did the math in my head and stepped back to observe her. I never got a bitch pregnant before, so I wasn't sure what thirteen weeks was supposed to look like but, to me, three ass months should have had a pudge.

"Why you ain't been tell me?" I asked.

She went and sat back on the bed as if she just didn't cause destruction all up and through this muthafucka.

"I just found out a couple of days ago. My cycle has always been irregular, so missing two periods was kind of the norm to me."

Hesitantly, I took a seat back on the bench where I was. "You wanna do this for real?" Again, I didn't want to ask for an abortion, but I wasn't against asking the prompting questions to get her in that direction.

"More than anything," she whispered with a glimmer of hope in her eyes.

Since abortion was officially off the table, my job tonight was to shut that hope of a relationship the fuck down by any means necessary. "I will do any and everything during this journey, but I wasn't asking if you were ready to have a baby. I was asking are you ready to be a single mother?"

She bit her bottom lip and, when she let go of it, it quivered. "Yes," she said so low that I had to strain my ears to hear it. "I'll reach out to an attorney tomorrow. Can you at least stay tonight?"

I guess she was coming to terms with my decision. I twisted my mouth in thought because I was about to tell her no. I did have business to handle but, when her floodgates opened and she started crying like it was hurting her, I agreed to say. I grabbed my other phone, the unbroken one, out of my pocket and shot Justice a quick message.

Isabella didn't want to do anything but cry, so I let her. I even went as far as to lie next to her in bed and hold her so that I could comfort her. When her whimpers turned to light snores, I snuck my ass out of the bed and went to pick up my broken phone from the floor. After sucking my teeth at the shattered screen, I placed the broken device into my pocket. I walked over to my closet to pack my shit. *Crazy ass bitch,* I thought to myself when I saw the mayhem she had brought upon my wardrobe. Whatever was salvageable, I packed away into suitcases and, what wasn't, I left right the fuck there. I made a mental note to get one of the cleaning crews to come and fix up what she had destroyed. When I zipped my last suitcase closed and rolled it out of the closet, the sun was starting to rise.

The rays peeked through the blinds and landed right on Isabella. She sat with her back pressed against our headboard. Her hair was wild, and her eyes were red and puffy from all of that damn crying.

"So, we're really done?" she asked.

She was staring at the nine suitcases I had already in the middle of the floor waiting to be taken out. The tenth one was at my side with the handle of it in my hand. I wrapped my fingers around the handle before pulling it beside the others.

"We are…"

I thought that when I said that shit that she would burst into a ball of tears again, but she didn't. She just shook her head up and down like she was finally coming to terms with everything. She didn't even bother to take her dress off before she pulled the cover over her and faced the window.

I stood there for a while just staring at her back. I saw it heaving up and down, so I knew that she was crying again, but it was inaudible. I handled what I told Justice I would and, now, it was time for me to make my exit. It took me five trips to get everything out. With the last trip heading out, I took the key to the house off my ring and placed it on the table in the foyer. There was so much shit on my to-do list for the day. I needed to know how the drop went, I needed to meet Doley to handle the score with Travis once and for all, and I needed to sit down with Alejandro.

CHAPTER 6

JUSTICE

Azul: I can't make it Ma. Fill me in tomorrow...

I sucked my teeth as I read the text from Azul's stupid ass. I had been so busy getting ready and making it to the garage that I was just now getting time to check my phone. I stood in the security booth of the loading dock by my damn self. Another mission was being completed by my lonesome because of what? This muthafucka had to tend to his privileged princess.

When I saw an 18-wheeler enter the garage, I stood from my seat and stood in the doorway of the security booth. Prepared, of course, a .40 Glock was tucked on my waist and a double barrel shotgun was on the table of the booth just in case.

Azul offered to have some workers wait around with me for protection but, honestly, after the last time bodies dropped when workers were around me, I didn't want the duty of being accountable for anyone else. The only extra people I had today were two men to help me offload the truck. Of course, they were still trained killers because Azul didn't want any repeats of what happened at the trap. We had cleaned out one of the suites so that the shipment could be placed there.

Beep, Beep, Beep!

The sound of a truck backing up and the white reverse lights were blinding, so I stepped fully out onto the dock so that I could get a clear view of the driver as they exited. When the door to the truck opened on the steel step, a pair of butter-colored constructs stepped out and the body that followed belonged to a hood nigga. I could tell in the gray sweatsuit that he wore that he was gutta. Naturally, I took a quick glance at his print and, whew, I could tell that thang was thanging. I noticed that a gun was in his pocket. I quickly walked to the side of the truck so that I could introduce myself.

"Sha I presume?"

He looked behind me with his thick brow dipped. "Yeah... where ya crew at little mama?"

"They coming down. I'm sure they saw you arrive on the cameras. I'm Justice by the way."

"Like the law?" he asked.

"Mmmm hmmm."

Instantly, I thought about the movie *Poetic Justice.* I had been hearing that line all of my life.

"A bitch named after the law and breaking it is fire as fuck to me."

I giggled slightly and took a moment to take in his appearance, as we waited for the two men to come down.

The back of both of his hands was tatted. The ink laid on a sepia-brown tone.

"You wanna page them or something? I don't do the waiting shit," he impatiently spat

I always had to in some shape or form experience an encounter with a rude-ass impatient nigga. It was like those were the only muthafuckas that God wanted to put in my presence. I pulled a walkie-talkie from my back pocket.

"Y'all asses not moving fast enough for me. I do have shit to do," I said into the device as I held down the side button.

In a matter of seconds, the walkie-talkie went off, "Sorry Boss Lady, Lonzo had to take a shit."

Sha looked at me and bust out laughing. "Not y'all having shitty ass workers. I woulda told the nigga while he was on the clock, ain't no time to shit. Since he wanna shit so bad, he needs a hot one in him and let the human body naturally do the rest."

The doors to the dock opened and these goofballs came walking out quickly. "Sorry Boss Lady," they said in unison.

"Uhh huhh," I was displeased and made no effort to hide it.

Sha opened the back of the truck and, when he did, a shitload of cleaning appliances like vacuums and carpet cleaners was what I was staring at. "The fuck is this?" I asked in an annoyed tone.

"Your muthafucking load. The fuck I look like driving a damn near nineteen-hour drive with wrapped coke in the back? The cleaning gear is a welcome onboard present from Bleek. Unscrew the back to the floor scrubbing machines, and there's work in there. There's also work in... man, just unscrew all that shit and you gone find your load."

I was impressed, and I knew that Zoo would be appreciative of the extra gifts that were given. I watched as Lonzo and his cousin offloaded the truck. Sha and I engaged in small talk while they made multiple trips. When he randomly rubbed his hands together, I took note of the wedding ring on his finger. I wondered what the future would hold for me and Azul. I knew that it was possible for a nigga to be in this game and tie a bitch down. What I didn't know was if Azul and I would ever make it to that point.

When the boys finished with their last trip, I watched as Sha closed the back of the truck.

"Well, have a safe drive back down," I said in a sweet tone.

"I'm flying love."

"Well, a safe flight."

"I appreciate it." He started walking towards the driver's side door but stopped to look at me before he hopped in. "Ya ass too pretty to be in the trenches alone. Tell ya nigga to tighten up. My gang doesn't play when they get a bitch like you. Do I have to send one of my homeboys ya way?"

I blushed and, although he was boldly crossing over the line of respect, I had to respect it. He was a big fish and he moved like one.

"Na, I'm good where I'm at."

He smirked at me. "You don't even believe that."

He hopped in the truck and pulled out of the garage before I could even offer a response. I blew out a sharp breath anxiously because like always, my nerves got the best of me anytime during a meet-up. When the rising sun's light started to peek into the garage, I hit the button on the wall to close it shut. My job was muthafucking done. I pulled my phone out of my back pocket.

Job done send my funds and Zoo... Fuck you

I added the middle finger emoji for a little dramatic effect. I was sure that when he woke up, he would have something to say because one thing about Azul, when I did a little razzle, his ass was gonna dazzle.

***

AZUL

After leaving the house, I knew that Justice would be pissed with me for not being there for the drop so, to avoid that drama for a bit, I booked myself a room. Some time and space were needed before I jumped head-first into another emotional encounter with a woman. Just how Isabella had lost her fucking mind when I told her that I was leaving her, I just knew that Justice would lose hers when I told her that I had a baby on the way. More importantly than anything, I needed to clear my head before meeting with Alejandro.

I freshened up before leaving my hotel room and going to meet him. I believed in breaking news over bread, whether good or bad. I sat in the booth at this soul food restaurant in Bedford Stuyvesant. Things with Isabella went better than I could have expected. That's why sitting down with Alejandro was mandatory. I had to make sure that there wasn't a price on my head for leaving his niece. I stood from my seat when he entered the restaurant. He wore this floral printed shirt with some white cargo shorts. The muthafucka always dressed like one of those vacation dads in the movies. He needed some Swag 101 classes and, over the years, I tried to get him together, but he was old and stuck in his ways.

"Azulllll..." he dragged as he reached his arms out to embrace me.

I guess ain't no love lost, I thought to myself as we hugged. When I tried to back away, he pressed firmly on my shoulder.

"She's my niece but she's my daughter, meng. This will be my great niece or nephew."

I got where he was coming from, but I was a grown man, and the sagging his nuts shit was gonna have to fly with someone else. "I respect what you're saying but respectfully... you gone have to bully someone else, *meng.*"

He put both hands on my shoulder and created some distance between us. His false teeth were big and intense. On his last trip back home to Mexico, he came back with that goofy bright-ass smile. The muthafucka came back with the wrong white bricks if you asked me. He let go of my shoulders and opened his palms towards the table.

"Shall we eat and discuss the end of our business?"

He took his seat, and I took mine. I just said that I wanted to meet with him, but I never mentioned what about. I guess Isabella told the man to cut ties with me.

"The end of business?" I questioned with a raised eyebrow, as he raised his hand to call over a waitress.

She borderline sprinted in our direction. Because he frequented the establishment we were in, I knew that she knew exactly who he was.

"Bring a bottle of 1942 Don Julio, my love," he ordered. He waited for her to scurry away before he finished speaking, "You do good business so, although I would have given you a hard time on your next two shipments, I would have continued business with you."

I sat back and listened to him intently. One thing about Alejandro was he was a man of few words so, anytime he spoke, I made sure to pay attention because there was always a lesson in his lyrics. He also was a businessman and put that first.

After the waitress came back with the bottle and two glasses filled with ice, he poured us up and finished speaking, "My cousin Manny put me in touch with Bleek. Me and the Dominicans have a very close-knit relationship.

If you're done here to start work with him, that's fine. I was already compensated for your departure."

"Word?"

He raised his cup to toast with me. "Word."

I couldn't help but let my deep dimples show with my smile. I knew that Bleek was the shit, the whole hood did, but this was really some boss shit.

"And Isabella?" I asked.

Business was handled, but that was his family. I didn't want to have to be on guard for the rest of my life but, if that was the case, I would rather be prepared for it. He placed his free hand on the back of his neck and rolled his head around like he was trying to relieve some of the stress from there.

"She's a woman, a pregnant woman that's emotional right now. She'll get over it."

I took a sip from my drink and welcomed the burn that traveled down. Everything was going right for me. I had solidified a new plug, and Doley was waiting in a nearby warehouse with Tremaine for me. I had every intention of letting Trav feel it for the stunt that he pulled. I needed to save the touchy discussion with Justice for later in the night. Getting to the warehouse was next on my list, and ending the night with Justice was the last stop to an eventful-filled day. I shared a couple more drinks with Alejandro before I dipped off.

***

The gate to the warehouse lifted and, when it did, I had to squint my eyes to adjust to the darkness. Doley was sitting on the trunk of a black Acura. My brow raised when I looked around and didn't see Tremaine tied to a chair. I walked up to Doley, and we did the handshake that we had since high school.

"Where the nigga at?" I asked.

Doley slid off the trunk and kicked it. When he did, I could hear what was muffled yelling.

"Man, open up the trunk and stop playing with that boy."

Doley popped the trunk open while I went to grab a nearby chair. By the time I turned around, Doley had him standing upright. When I looked into the boy's face, I could see the stained trails that the tears he must have shed on the way down left behind. The nigga was soft as fuck, and I really hated that I had to do it to him. Doley pushed him down to sit in the chair by his shoulder. There was no need to tie him to the muthafucka because he had duct tape wrapped around his ankles and his wrist. I saw his lips quivering under the piece of duct tape that covered his mouth.

"What you wanna do Zoo?" Doley asked as he pulled a wrapped blunt from behind his ear and lit it up.

After taking a pull, he handed it to me and I took one. I needed that shit really bad; I didn't even get a chance to fill Do into what the fuck was going on with me.

"Isabella pregnant," I blurted out before handing him back the blunt.

His eyes opened wide as fuck. "Dead ass?"

I shook my head up and down, as he took a pull and handed the blunt back to me. "Jus gone flip the fuck out," I said after I exhaled.

"Yeah, she is… you better get ya block game ready 'cause she gone try and take ya muthafucking head off."

I sighed just thinking about how Justice would react to the news. Tremaine was looking in between me and Doley quickly. We were just casually having a conversation above him as if he wasn't even there.

113

"Doley, Facetime this nigga bruva. Let's get this shit done."

He passed me the phone, and the phone rang for a bit before Trav picked up.

"Yo Tre—" Trav looked at the screen and saw it was me. "Zoo… fuck you want nigga?"

"I want you to tell me if I should clip ya baby bruva or not?"

I flipped the camera around to show his ass the little nigga in the chair. I could see Trav use his hand to swipe over his face. He stood quiet on the line and, when he didn't seem moved to me, I snatched the piece of duct tape off his brother's mouth.

"Travis! They gone kill me, man. Travis! Travis!"

"Aight aight…" I slapped the piece of duct tape back over his mouth, "I'ma give you an address and you gone pull up over there and, then, I'll let ya little bruva go."

This muthafucka looked me dead in the face and shook his head. "Yeah, Tre, they are gonna kill you. Zoo, I'ma catch you in the town."

Before I could respond, that nigga hung up on me.

"Damn, that's cold as fuck," Doley said as he cocked his gun back.

The boy in the chair jumped at the sound it made. Tears and snot rushed down his face as he practically shook in the chair.

"Ahhh, you about to die little nigga," Doley said as he placed the gun on Tremaine's shoulder. He loved getting his hands dirty. I didn't mind but, every time he took a life, I knew that he enjoyed it.

"Yo Doley, chill out."

He was taunting the little nigga, and I just needed a moment to think. I would be a father soon and this kid obviously had a brother that didn't give a fuck about him.

"You ever been to DR?" I asked Tremaine before snatching the duct tape off his mouth.

Doley threw his hands in the air like he was fed up. I didn't have it in me for him to kill the nigga. I did some homework on the boy and, overall, he was a good kid. From the jump, I never had intentions of killing him; I just wanted to draw his brother out. Since my plan failed, I didn't see the sense in falling through with the plan. What I could do was make it look like I did though.

"No, I never been," he said in between sniffles.

I knew that I could call in a favor with Bleek. I hated unnecessary bloodshed, and this shit was it. This boy didn't know shit about the game and that was clear in how he was folding with just being kidnapped.

"I did that long-ass drive for nothing? This some bullshit," Doley said before he popped the locks on the car and grabbed a bag out of it. He tossed me the keys, and I caught them mid-air.

"Do shit how you want to do shit. I'm going the fuck home." He sucked his teeth before exiting the warehouse.

"So, you not gone kill me?"

I let Tremaine's words linger in the air for a moment because honestly, the simple thing to do would be to off the little nigga. That nagging ass feeling in my gut wouldn't let me though. I chuckled to myself because I knew that if I had Justice in this warehouse with me, she would have blown the little nigga's head off without a second thought. She was thorough as fuck and, honestly, the more gangsta one of us two. She was solely responsible for putting in pain in this drug game, and I loved her to death for it. I made a mental note to text Doley later to let him know to keep me sparing Tremaine away from Justice. Boss Lady put in for the hit, and I wasn't executing it. I just knew that she wouldn't let me live the shit down if she ever knew.

"Na, I ain't gone kill you, kid," I said as I pulled my trap phone out. I texted the address of the warehouse to my cleaner on-call. I would explain to him later how I needed him to stage a murder and to make it look good. I had planned on getting those photos out to Travis. Just in case he was playing that hard shit on the phone, he was going to feel this shit.

I checked the watch on my wrist and mentally calculated how much extra time I had to spare before I had to make it home to Justice. With so much that still needed to be done, I made the rash decision to get around to Justice within a couple of days. I made one call; I needed Bleek's help and I hated that so early on in our business relationship that I was reaching out for favors, but I had the feeling that he wouldn't tell a nigga no. He had handled my dealings with Alejandro off just knowing that it was a tough situation for me, so I knew that this situation would be light for him. The phone rang once in my ear.

"It better be urgent if you're calling me…" his voice was so monotone.

"I need a favor."

CHAPTER 7

DOLEY

I still couldn't believe that Zoo just let the little muthafucka run scot-free like that. I hated unfinished business and, for the past five days, all I kept thinking about was the loose end that Zoo let voluntarily get away. I kept reading over his text message because not only did he let the nigga go, but he wanted me to hide the shit from Justice as well. What Trav did at that trap house was personal as fuck, and she was the one that experienced it. Sis was so gutta that I was sure she would have put a hot one in Zoo himself for not taking care of business.

I still hadn't responded to him because I was still in my feelings over the shit. I took that long ass drive to go and get the nigga, and for what? For him to get handed a lifelong vacation and a fresh start. That nigga saw my damn face and knew my damn name. Not for nothing if anything ever came back to me, then I wouldn't hesitate to off my brother. I sucked my teeth before locking my phone and placing it in the empty space beside me.

I sat on a plum-colored suede sectional that sat in the middle of Imon's living room stuck in thought. Her little ass had just been posting away on her Instagram account without responding to a nigga and, to be honest, the shit was driving me crazy. About three hours ago, she posted a boomerang of her walking around an airport and the location tag said Miami International Airport; that's when I made my way to her crib. All it took was for one post of her hand over the sandy beach with this nice ass ring on her finger that captioned *I'ma let y'all in my business just this once* for me to act out of character. Imon was gorgeous and smart as hell. She majored in Business with an Accounting minor. Straight out of college, she landed one of those good ass jobs on Wall Street.

When I heard keys jiggling in her front door, I sat my damn near empty Corona bottle on the floor and waited. I felt like Mr. Biggs the way I was waiting in the dark for my bitch to make her arrival, but I didn't give a fuck. I needed to know where the fuck she had gotten that ring from and why she thought that she could play in my face by posting it. What had me more pissed than the actual picture was her girl group of hoe-ass friends in the comment section with their *yesss* and *as he should* remarks because who the fuck was he when it damn sure wasn't me.

The sound of her rolling her suitcase over the hardwood floors was hyping me up. I had been waiting five ass days to address this shit and my moment was finally here. She was looking too good on vacation and, although I was mad, I missed her.

"Yes girl, next trip is Aruba. Hell yeah, we going," she chuckled.

I guess she was on the phone. The light in the room turned on, and I had to adjust my eyes because I was just sitting in the dark for the past three hours.

"Oh, my God! David, what the hell!" she screamed.

"Girl, let me call you back," she said into the phone before hanging up. "What the hell are you doing here sitting in the dark?"

I stood from the chair and closed the space between us. "Put your hand out."

"What?" she asked with an arched raised eyebrow.

I knew that my request may have sounded insane. Before I repeated myself, I just looked at her cute ass. She wore this sundress that had a split on the right-hand side. Her chocolate skin was glistening. Where I was tatted up like a subway in Harlem, she was ink free and I loved that. She was really the yin to my yang, and I was finally coming to terms with me having to express that shit. I didn't know how much longer I could go on with her at my side if I didn't express just how much she meant to me.

I could tell that she had a little bit too much fun on her vacation because the lace to her jet-black 40-inch bust down was lifting a bit. I shook my head to clear my thoughts and repeated myself, "Put your hand out."

She put out her right hand.

"Not that one."

She then put out her left hand and, as soon as she did, I looked down at the iced-out ring and popped the shit out of her hand how my moms used to do when I would touch anything in the store as a little boy.

"Ouchhhhh," she said as she quickly pulled her hand back in and placed it at her side.

"Ouch is muthafucking right. That's what I said when I saw ya lame-ass post. Who got you that fucking ring?"

"Not you jealoussss…" she said in a drag before smirking.

"*Not you jealoussss*," I mimicked her. "Ain't nobody fucking jealous."

I knew that my pop must have hurt her ass because she was shaking the pain out of that damn hand. I walked back to the couch, took a seat, and downed the last bit of suds that was in my beer bottle.

"Yeah, you are because why are you here then?"

"A nigga miss you." I said the shit because I did but, more than anything, I was territorial and she knew that.

We played this toxic ass game where I would piss her off and, then, she would do what I would call hoe shit, but it really wasn't shit but her seeking attention. She would always try and get a rise out of my ass. It was like she lived off that shit for real.

"Ohhh… you missed me, huh?" she asked as she slid out of her Jesus walks sandals before tip-toeing in my direction.

"Mmm hmmm," I grumbled.

"What did you miss about me?" she said all sexy and shit as she straddled me.

I tried my hardest to not let her feel me brick up beneath her. "Who got you that ring Imon?" I asked.

She wasn't about to use that golden box to switch the topic at hand. When she started kissing my neck and nibbled on my ear, I grabbed a handful of her ass. "Sssss…" I couldn't help but hiss because she knew just what I liked.

She put her knees into the couch and lifted her weight off me to pull my tool out. I should have known she didn't have any panties on because that's just how she rolled. When she slid onto my pole, I couldn't help but brace myself at her gushy insides.

"What did you miss about me?" she asked as she rotated her hips and grinded, doing that thing that felt good to her clit but weird as fuck to me.

I grabbed her hair and pulled as I thrusted from underneath her. She grabbed the back of the couch and started moaning as she looked up to the ceiling. "Bounce on the dick."

She did what she was told and we met thrust for thrust. When I saw the lace to her hair start to peel more, I smiled sinisterly. I knew that she had taken her time putting this bitch on because this wasn't the hairstyle that she had left my crib with.

"I'll snatch this muthafucka off right now if you don't tell me who got you that ring." I wrapped the hair around my hand and tightened my grip.

"David, are you fucking serious?" she said with an annoyed tone as she stopped riding.

"Keep riding this dick. Tell me what nigga I gotta catch a flight and kill since he thinks it's cute to buy *my* bitch shit."

She bit her bottom lip as she continued to ride me. The eye contact she was giving me was about to make me bust a load, but I held it down. When she took too long to answer, I started pulling that hair back.

"Okay, okay. Turn the gun on yourself, you bought it! I got it with the money you gave me."

"You like making a nigga jealous huh, Mon?"

I let go of her hair and grabbed her neck. I didn't even give her the chance to answer me because I kissed her deeply. This bitch was gone have me flip out for real one day. The only thing that I could think of was going forward, I needed to start tending to her needs and showing her that although I had the most trouble with showing her, I did really appreciate her ass. Our tongues danced with one another as

I caressed her insides with my wood. She was moaning in my mouth, and I knew that she was about to cum by the way her eyebrows dipped. When her mouth fell into an o, I knew I had her ass.

"I'm cumm—"

"You cumming, I know. Cum for daddy."

As soon as she coated my shaft with her nectar, I exploded inside of her.

"I love you, David. I just want you to act right," she admitted.

"I know, I got you." I kissed her forehead. "Call ya friend back and let her know that you going to Aruba with ya nigga. That hoe trip is canceled."

She slapped my chest and let out a laugh that had me laughing too. It was the way her dimples deepened when she exposed those pearly whites for me.

"When are we going?"

I scrunched my face up as I thought about when a good time would be to go. Being that Zoo had pissed me off and I was sure he needed time with Justice with that whole baby on the way shit, taking a vacation right now would be great.

"Book it for tomorrow."

"Davey, I have work tomorrow."

I hated it when she called me that shit but only a nickname like that could fly with her. I used the back of my hand and touched her forehead. "Feel like a fever to me. I'ma pay you for your time."

She smiled all flirtatiously. Good girls loved when a hood nigga would pay them for their time and, every time she missed work because of me, she was compensated.

"Pay me in this." She did one of those Kegels that had me back on brick.

Nasty ass bitch, I thought to myself when she slid off of me and dropped to her knees to suck me off. She didn't even care that my seeds were spilling out of her ass. I laid my head back on the couch and enjoyed the superb blow job. I was content with showing my feelings a little just to have us in a better space. I closed my eyes as I tried to picture us having this exact moment on someone's beach.

***

JUSTICE

The words echoed off the walls at full speed. *Isabella is pregnant.* Of all things this muthafucka could have said out his mouth after letting me know that he had left his wife of nine years, I didn't expect that shit.

"Jus…"

I ignored his ass as I sat on my couch just twiddling my thumbs.

"Justice... I left. We're not together anymore so that battle is handled."

I heard what he was saying and I got it. At least he finally did leave her but, by leaving her, we would now be gaining a child that he had to be responsible for. Even though he had a whole wife, I still always saw myself being the first and only to bare his children. Instantly, I felt sick to my stomach. I didn't want to turn bitch but, as soon as my eyes watered up, I couldn't help myself. As quickly as my eyes watered, the tears streamed down my face.

"Justice..."

Azul got on his knees in front of me and started cleaning my face. Small whimpers escaped my mouth because I was truly the fuck tired. I was finally getting the nigga and look what it was coming with. I felt like I wanted to scream, but I didn't because what would that have fixed? Me screaming and tearing up my place just to get some rage out wouldn't change the fact that another woman would be carrying the love of my life's child. Only for a moment did I think about killing the bitch, but the love I had for Azul wouldn't allow me to hurt a piece of him. He dressed my face in kisses as he kept telling me sorry. That stupid ass word wasn't going to change anything either.

"I need space," I managed to say once I got my tears under control.

"No..."

I looked Azul in the eyes and, instantly, rage filled me. I didn't ask for much. Come to think of it, I didn't ask for shit but the absolute one thing that I did ask for, he couldn't even deliver. Almost ten fucking years ago, I told Azul that I would stick by his side after marrying Isabella because I understood the sacrifice that he was making. THE ONLY thing I asked was that he not make any children. Asking him not to fuck his own wife was a reach and I knew that, but I just asked that he use protection because he hadn't and never had used any between us. Hearing him tell me no to me wanting space infuriated me so damn much that I balled my right fist up and clocked his ass. I hit him so hard that he fell over from his knees and onto the floor.

"I asked you not to get the bitch pregnant and what the fuck you do! The least you can do is give me my muthafucking space!" I yelled as I stood from the couch and stepped over him.

I walked to the closet in my room and pulled down a duffle bag. I heard him quickly scurry from the floor and quickly make his way in my direction. I had to remember that I just put my hands on him and, when I did that shit, I opened the door to possibly get hit back, so I turned around and stood in a fighting stance as I waited for him just in case.

He entered the closet holding his right eye. His eyes were filled with tears, and I couldn't tell if it was from anger because I hit him or from regret that he had disappointed me once again.

"Justice, I don't need space. I need you."

"Oh, you still think that I give a fuck about what you need? WHO CARES ABOUT WHAT JUSTICE NEEDS?" I beat on my chest with the last part because I had been on the back burner for damn near a decade, and the shit was draining. I turned around and started snatching clothes off hangers and tossing them in a duffle bag.

"Please," his voice cracked and, when it did, I turned around to face him. He looked like a small boy, the boy I had met in seventh grade. "Ma, I don't know how to be without you…"

"Ughhhh…" I groaned as I used the back of my hand to wipe the falling tears from my face.

I dropped the duffle bag and the clothes I had in my hand and just took a seat on the carpeted floor. My mind was racing and I just needed a moment of stillness. I exhaled as I pulled my knees into my chest and wrapped my arms around my legs. Once I laid my head on my knees, I let my emotions out freely. Feeling Azul's strong arms wrapped around me made me feel weaker, only because I knew that I would stay. I loved the nigga with everything in me, so rolling with the punches was something that I had become accustomed to. It didn't matter if they were haymakers or not.

"Baby I'm sorry." He kissed the sides of my neck.

Usually, that little move right there would have had me wetter than a water slide, but it was giving desert storm down there.

"I'm sorry... I'm sorry... I'm sorry..." He kissed me repeatedly and just held me.

It felt like he held me for hours. I cried, real bad and, when no more tears would come out, I just sat in silence and he let me. When we finally got up from the floor, I decided on leaving those emotions about the shit right there in that spot. I was making the decision to move forward, and it made no sense to bicker or dwell on what was now our lifelong situation. I didn't even bother to clean up the closet because I was sure that he would eventually.

As I walked to my bed, I made a mental note to be more diligent with taking my birth control because the last thing that I wanted was to be pregnant.

CHAPTER 8

JUSTICE

7 MONTHS LATER...

I sat on the closed toilet seat with my knees touching. I was pretty sure that the bathroom walls were spinning around me because of the positive pregnancy test I had in my hand.

"Jus..."

The light tap on the door that followed his concerning tone infuriated me.

"Zoo, leave me alone."

We still had boxes all over the house from just moving in. I couldn't even enjoy the feeling of a new home without a dark ass cloud hovering over me.

Knock, knock!

"Justice," he added a little bass in his voice this time that I didn't give a fuck about.

I placed the positive pregnancy test on the sink's counter next to the other three. He was excited and, for the life of me, I couldn't figure out why. Isabella was due any damn day. I didn't get how he could be okay with the thought of ghetto twins. Ghetto twins were kids close in age that had two different mothers. If I kept this baby, our child and his with Isabella would be months apart. The thought alone made me sick to my stomach.

I heard Azul sigh and that was when I thought of how all of this must have been weighing on him.

"Jus... Ma, this isn't a bad thing."

I wasn't a baby kind of bitch to begin with. So, I couldn't imagine what it would be like to have two babies yelling their heads off. Of course, a product of Azul would be loved enormously by me just off the strength of how much I loved him. Still, I didn't have that motherly aura to me. My own niece didn't fuck with me for real. My sister used to say that I might as well hang my ovaries up in the closet because I wouldn't have any use for them.

"Justice..."

I saw the knob to the locked door wiggling.

"I'm just going to sit out here until you come out. It's not like you gone be in there all night."

I heard his back slide down the door, and his shadow covered the small trim of light peeking from under the door. If I wanted to, I could have camped out in that damn bathroom. We had more than enough towels in the bathroom closet for me to make a comfortable ass pad in our spacious master bathtub. I quickly stood from the toilet and opened the closet door.

"Justice, if you trying to sleep in that muthafucking tub, I'm gone kick the door down and sleep beside you."

I sucked my teeth because I was sure that me saying how I would sleep in this big ass tub when we were viewing the house played in his head. Since it made no sense to hide out any longer, I swung the bathroom door open in frustration. He quickly stood from the floor and to his feet. His thick brows dipped and a saddened expression graced his face. I knew that I looked like shit. I had been sick all damn day and, for the past week, I wasn't able to keep anything down.

"What Azul?" I had a big-ass attitude, and the pity look he was giving me was driving me insane.

***

AZUL

"What Azul?"

Justice's pouty little mouth was fixed in a tight scowl. I quickly imagined her doing that same motherly tight lip when telling our future child to stop doing something. Her heart was warm and pure, but my little baby was mean as hell. I already knew that she would be one of those mamas where our kid's friends would have to ask permission for shit. I could see a teenage mixture version of us saying, *"Ask my mom if I can go."*

I was dazed thinking of our future, which pissed her the hell off. She leaned her head forward as to silently say *what* again. I watched her attempt to push wild hair out of her face but, from sweating so much from being sick for the past week, her normal silky strands were puffy as hell.

"Let's go and get something to eat. You need to put something on your stomach."

She had been hiding out in that damn bathroom for the past four hours. She took one pregnancy test in front of me and, before I could even celebrate, she immediately brought up getting an abortion. Before I could express how against her decision I was, she pushed my ass out of the bathroom, slammed the door in my face, and locked it.

"I don't want to eat."

She looked sick in the face, and I'd be damned if she didn't eat. She had an attitude and I understood that, but starving herself wasn't the answer. She wanted to discuss abortion, and I told her that it was nothing to discuss. Not wanting to bring up the conversation that had her lock herself in the bathroom to begin with, I focused back on what we should eat for dinner. We hadn't unpacked the pots and pan sets that she had purchased and I knew damn well like me, she didn't feel like cooking.

"Oxtails?" I questioned.

Her face lit up and that made me smile.

"Extra gravy on the rice?" she asked with the corners of her mouth turned up.

"You wouldn't have it any other way."

She walked over to our king-sized bed and hopped in. "Bring me back a pineapple soda too," she added.

It had been damn near two weeks since I saw her go outside. "Na, Ma, slip your feet in those ugly ass big teddy bear slippers and let's go."

She kissed those damn teeth and threw her head back in annoyance. I didn't see how she had any muthafucking teeth left as much as she sucked those pearly straight things.

"You need air Ma," I added as I walked over to the bed and held one of her slippers up for her to put her foot in.

When she dangled her foot off the side of our bed, I kissed the bottom of her chubby foot before putting her slipper on. I did the same to the other foot. I loved every ounce of her body, and there wasn't a piece of her that I didn't have in my mouth before.

***

JUSTICE

I wiggled my loose toes on the dashboard of Azul's Tesla. Smoothly, he maneuvered through the streets of Queens. This one Jamaican restaurant had been around since we were kids, and they had the best oxtails in town. Azul, Doley, and I would hop on bikes and ride from East New York to Queens just to get a platter of food from them.

"Come on, you got your little toe marks on my damn dashboard."

I slapped my whole foot on the windshield and giggled when he caught a fit. He grabbed my hand and kissed the back of it. Azul was always affectionate but, for the first time in his life, he seemed at peace. Why wouldn't he be? Money was great, our home life was amazing, Isabella was finally not being a headache and he had a bad bitch at his side.

The block of the restaurant was active. Being that it was a Friday night, I knew that everyone was waiting on their Jamaican food. I was glad that on the drive over, Azul had called the order in. He parked in front of a fire hydrant and kissed my lips quickly before exiting the car. As he walked inside, he looked back and gave me a wink.

The crowded lobby of the restaurant made me uneasy. I didn't have a clear view of my man and I didn't like that. I squinted my eyes a bit, and I was able to see Azul's bean head moving around in the crowd. Seeing that he was making his exit relaxed me. I turned up the radio and sang along with Beyonce.

I've been watching for the signs

Took a trip to clear my mind, oh

Now I'm even more lost

And you're still so fine, oh my, oh my

Been having conversations about breakups and separations

I'm not feeling like myself since the baby

Are we gonna even make it? Oh...

***

AZUL

I pushed my way through the crowd to make it to the front counter.

"Order 213!" the boy behind the counter called out.

I watched another nigga push his way to the front to get his food. It was hot as fuck in the store, and I was just glad that I had called ahead with my order.

"Azul..."

Janice, the owner, rushed around the counter to give me a hug. When I was a young boy, I used to clean up around the restaurant to stay out of trouble. I would hop on my bike and ride for fifteen minutes just to get peace of mind. I hugged Janice tightly before letting her go.

"The call in order for Zoo was you?" she asked.

"Yeah."

She grabbed a bag off the counter and handed it to me. "You must have that mean ass Justice with you. I could tell from the jerk, BBQ, and oxtail gravy on the rice and that pineapple soda."

I smiled because these were the memories that me and Justice could share with our child. When we were younger, Janice used to tell Justice that when she became a grown woman, she would have the ugliest face if she kept screwing up her face as a child. I shook off the nostalgic feel that came with being around Janice. Her long locs now had strands of gray. The entire front section of that stress belonged to me, the sides belonged to Doley and that gray in the back of her kitchen belonged to Justice. Janice had kids of her own, but they walked the straight and narrow. She had a soft spot for delinquents, and that's exactly what we were.

"She's waiting in the car," I said because I knew that Janice would be excited to see Justice.

"Ahhh," she squealed, "let me come out and see my baby." She took off her apron and tossed it onto the counter. She started following me out, but one of her workers called out to her.

"Wait for me, Azul. I'll be out in a bit."

"Okay, I'm parked right out front."

The front door was wide open, and it was needed. The tiny corner restaurant was hot as hell from all of the people packed inside. My ass started sweating just standing there talking with Janice. Right when I was about to get some fresh air from being outside, my phone rang. It was too damn loud in the store to answer Isabella, so I shot the call to voicemail. I would call her back when I got into the car. I was sure the call was for a food request that I would just have to order for her via Uber Eats. My phone vibrated in my hand again, and it was Isabella texting me.

Isabella: THE BABY IS COMING

I was probably showing all of my thirty-two pearly whites. I put a little pep in my step with my exit. I smirked as I watched Justice sing her heart out. I could tell what song was playing by the bass on my speakers.

"I just wanna say you're mine, you're mine," I lightly sang as I let my legs carry me toward the car.

That was going to be our wedding song for sure. She played the shit once a day, and I learned all the words because of it. Over the past months, she had been hinting at tying the knot. Being that my divorce was now finalized, she had no idea how much I wanted to wife her ass. I had already gotten the ring and everything; I was just waiting on the perfect moment to pop the question.

"Yo Zoo!"

I quickly turned to my left and, when I did, the nose to a .45 was pointing in my direction. I thought about reaching for my gun, but I realized that I had left it in the car when I was rushing to get the food. With just menacing eyes peeking through the open section of the ski mask, I knew that those dark, hating ass pupils belonged to Trav. I might as well call the nigga Pooh Shiesty because he always had a ski mask tucked away somewhere.

It was hot as fuck outside, and his weird ass was masked up and ready. I wasn't even checking my surroundings when I walked into the damn restaurant, so I was sure that's probably when he noticed me and waited. I knew that he wanted blood to shed for the staged photos that

I had sent to him. My cleaner did a damn good job, and Tremaine did his part by posing as the dead in the photos before I had him shipped off to the Dominican Republic.

Before I could try and make a dash for cover, two shots went off. I felt a hot ass impact pierce my stomach and it put me down. I had never been shot before and I wasn't sure if one bullet hit my spine or if I was just in shock, but I couldn't move my legs. I stared up at the dark sky as I felt the blood pouring out of my stomach.

"NYPD STOP!"

I heard feet running pass my head.

"Azul!!!" Justice screamed. In seconds, she appeared within eyesight. "Zoo." I felt her push her small hands on my stomach. "Zoo, you okay baby. You're okay."

The fear I saw in her eyes and the tears and snot that ran down her face let me know that I was indeed not okay.

"Azul!" Janice had the horrifying scream of a mother seeing her son bleeding out on the concrete.

I kept thinking how bad I was about to go out. Quickly, I remembered that Isabella had texted me that the baby was on the way.

Boom! Boom! Boom! Boom!

Justice laid her body on top of mine as more shots rang out.

"NYPD, get down, get down," I heard in the distance.

She quickly lifted from lying across me to stare down the street. She was squinting. I made a mental note to get my baby some glasses if I made it out of this shit.

"Yes, kill his ass!" I heard Janice yell out.

"Just hold on, you hear those sirens. The ambulance is coming," Justice quickly said to me.

It was a damn shame that I was about to be on somebody's operating table when my daughter was going to be born. I had to let Justice know that Isabella was having the baby, just in case I didn't make it out of this.

"Jus…" I was able to get out before I started coughing up blood.

"Azul, don't speak, please save your energy," I heard Janice say.

I bit down on my bottom lip hard because now, I was starting to feel the agonizing pain in my stomach. "Fuckkkk!" I roared as the pain radiated within me.

"Azul! Azul!"

I could hear Justice yelling, but everything went dark.

"Azul…"

CHAPTER 9

JUSTICE

The smell of a hospital was something that would always be stuck in the back of my nostrils somewhere. I sat with my legs shaking, eagerly, impatiently, and worriedly. *How much longer is this surgery going to take?* I wondered while I sat wringing out my hands. Janice sat beside me praying. Azul was going to pull through this shit. He had to.

"Yo what the fuck happened?"

Doley rushed into the waiting room. His light-skinned face was flustered. I called him on our way to the hospital and just told him that Azul was hurt; I didn't go into specifics. Janice stood from her seat and ran and hugged him. He embraced her and stared at me, waiting for a response. His thick brows were scrunched in anger and the look in his eye just told me that he was about to make the streets bleed for this one.

155

"Ummm…" I started to say but I couldn't get the words out.

Janice let go of Doley, and he came to console me. I cried into his chest. Finally, I released all I had been holding on to for the past couple of hours. I knew that life changed in a blink of an eye, but how quickly did I muthafucking blink for it to change up this drastically on me?

"He shot him, Do. In the damn stomach, it looked so bad. I don't think he's going to make it."

I shook in his embrace because losing Azul would be the end of the world for me. His blood tainted the palms of my hand and also my nightshirt. Instantly, I thought about the baby in my stomach; I had to keep it. Of course, Azul would have his and Isabella's child to carry on his legacy, but I needed the little peanut in my stomach that would be a forever connection for me and Zoo.

"Who the fuck is him?" Doley asked.

"Trav..."

I heard Doley sigh deeply. I just knew that his trigger finger was itching.

"Ima torture that nigga slowly and then kill his ass."

"The cops already killed him..."

He let out a deep breath before breaking our embrace. "He gone be good." His hazel eyes looked deep into mine. "He the goat, he not going out bad like that."

I shook my head up and down because he was right. Azul was the shit, and I knew that my baby was going to push through this shit.

"The family of Mr. Azul Jones!" a doctor called out, catching the attention of me, Doley, and Janice.

As a group, we quickly closed in the space between him and us.

"Yes," I answered.

The doctor had a motionless face. I couldn't read him and I hated that. I was sure that years in his profession molded this expression to be his resting face. The gray hair on top of his head was stress from his job, I knew it. If I had the task of delivering bad news to families, my entire head would be gray too.

"Spit that shit out. Is my brother good?"

Doley didn't have any patience. I didn't either but mine were at least slim, his was nonexistent. I inhaled deeply to prepare myself and, instantly, a wave of heat washed over me and the room started to spin.

"Nurse!" I heard the doctor yell before I hit the cold tiled floor beneath me.

***

DOLEY

I sat at my brother's bedside, waiting on him to wake up. I almost yoked that doctor up in the waiting room because it was taking him forever to tell us what was up with Zoo. They did the surgery but, where the bullet was, they couldn't pull it out without causing more damage. I was just glad that my bro was alive. We could deal with the risks of the bullet moving around later. He was breathing today, and that was a win in my eyes.

He started to stir in his sleep, so I knew that he would be waking soon. The first thing that he was gonna do was to ask about Justice, and I didn't quite know how I could explain that one. They hauled her ass off to emergency surgery after she fainted in the waiting room. I explained to the doctor that I was her brother, so he disclosed all of her medical information to me.

She had passed out because her right fallopian tube had ruptured and, to top that off, she was pregnant with an ectopic pregnancy. I had been splitting my time between her room and Zoo's room to see who would wake up first. It looked like Zoo was the winner of that race. The doctors couldn't do shit to save their baby because it wasn't where it was supposed to be to begin with. I didn't know if Zoo knew about her pregnancy. After all, the doctor did say that she was early on.

"Whatchu sitting there all serious for nigga?"

Man, if I was the mushy soft type, I would have hugged his ass for real. It was good to hear his voice. "Was waiting on you to open those eyes nigga. Welcome back to the land of the living."

He sucked his teeth together and just laid there for a bit. I wondered what was going through his mind as he stared up at the iridescent hospital lights.

"What's on your mind, bro?"

"Trav gotta go and, honestly, I should have deaded his brother."

I wasn't into the *I told you so* but I knew that. What was done, was done. Trav was gone, and Zoo already gave his little brother the green light to start fresh, so it didn't make any sense to snatch that from him now.

"It's already done."

"Where's Justice? And Janice?" he asked.

"I sent Janice's old ass home. She was head slumped over in the chair over there waiting for you to wake up. I told her I would text her to update her when you were up."

"And Justice?"

And here came the hard part. "She's a few rooms down."

He tried to sit up, so I stood and walked over to assist him.

"Whatchu mean a few rooms down?"

"She passed out when the doctor came out to tell us about you."

"How is the baby? How is she?"

Whew, I'm glad this nigga knows, I thought as a sense of relief washed over me.

Instantly, that relief was replaced with sorrow. I had to break the news to my boy that their baby didn't make it. Zoo was my brother without a doubt but, Justice, she was baby sis. I had known her first, and she was the one who had made it possible for me to eat by bringing me to the table. Zoo must have picked up on my facial expression. I was hard as stone, but shit like the emotions that came with loss was something that I couldn't mask. I really felt like the message was something that I shouldn't relay but I knew that although

162

he had just been shot, he would have to be there emotionally for Justice.

"The baby didn't make it."

He bit his bottom lip and the muthafucka started laughing. I didn't find the humor in none of this shit.

"Isabella is in labor by the way. Well, was. I don't even fucking know if she had the baby. That's the last text I got before all of this bullshit."

If it wasn't one thing, it was another. Knowing that, I appreciated it ten times more that my boy had pulled through. It would have been a damn shame if his daughter's birthday was the day he had died.

"I can tap in with Alejandro to check on Isabella and my niece. You need to rest up, ain't shit you can do about not being there when she was born. Ain't shit you can do about any of this."

"Right now, I can be there for Justice though. Tell a nurse to bring a wheelchair. I need to make sure my baby is good."

"Yeah, I can do that. She can help you get in that shit though 'cause I love you, bro, but I ain't trynna have ya black ass moon me."

He laughed, as I pointed at the hospital gown that he was dressed in. A nurse quickly came to my aide as soon as I walked into the hall. I gave her Zoo's request and added one of my own before making my exit.

"Tell my brother that I'll be back." I took my phone out of my pocket to give Alejandro a call. I didn't even know what hospital Isabella was in.

***

JUSTICE

I laid on my side in a fetal position. For me not to want something so bad, I was heartbroken that I didn't have it anymore and that the chances of ever having it again were slim to none. I buried my face into the white hospital pillowcase and let a scream out. My room door opened, and I just knew that it was one of the nurses to either check on me or stick me with some shit to calm me. Or it could have been worst, the hospital's therapist, to talk about my loss and the best ways to deal with postpartum stress.

"Leave me alone," I groaned out without turning around to face the door.

"Ma, you've been raising hell?"

I almost broke my damn neck when I turned around. "Azul."

The nurse couldn't wheel him over to me fast enough. Once he was at my bedside, I was leaning over the railing to shower him in kisses. It didn't matter that it was hurting my stomach in the process.

"Move over."

Without hesitation, I followed his order and scooted out of the way.

"Can you help me up there?" he asked the nurse.

She twisted her tight ass mouth in uncertainty before she answered, "Usually, we don't allow—"

The way we both cut eyes at her stopped her mid-sentence. She lowered the arm of my bed and helped him inside. After lifting the arm back up, she walked out to give us some privacy. I laid my head on his shoulder because I was too afraid to lie across his chest with how his entire midsection was bandaged up.

"Three more inches this way and I would have had a shit bag attached to me for the rest of my life." He showed on his stomach the place that would have really changed his life forever. "You was gonna rock with a nigga with a doo-doo bag attached to him?"

He had no idea how nothing in this world could stop me from fucking with him. "I would have been changing it and everything. Nothing can get me off your heels, Mr. Jones."

"The vibe is mutual soon-to-be, Mrs. Jones."

I blushed at his comment because I didn't doubt that one day, I would be his wife. I just preferred that the ink dried on his divorce decree before doing so. There was a long silence and I was sure we were both stuck in our thoughts.

"You know we can try again, right?"

I didn't even think of telling him what had happened but I see that Doley had done the job for me. In an instant, my eyes watered. "I have a forty-five percent chance of carrying to full term."

"We always beat the odds Ma." He kissed the top of my head and, although we were both down bad right now, I knew that one day, things would be better.

CHAPTER 10

ISABELLA

I was a mom. I laid in the hospital bed just taking the shit in. Eight hours in labor was excruciating but all worth it in the end. Aliana Jones was perfect in every way. My Tío was by my side the entire time. I didn't see how he could calmly watch as my pussy turned inside out with giving birth to my daughter. I had sent him home to get some proper rest because I was sure that the hospital chair he had been napping in was a lot for his aging body. I was taking a moment for myself. Giving birth took a toll on my body and trying to breastfeed was stressing me out.

The nurses took Aliana to the nursey to give me what they called a *mommy break*. Bonding after birth was important, but it was clear that I was getting overwhelmed with struggling to get her to latch on to nurse her. I flipped through the channels on the television while scrolling through my phone. Azul had yet to call or text me back, and I was pissed about it. He had missed the birth of our daughter and a huge part of me blamed his new bitch.

In such a short time, so much had changed with us, so I was still adjusting. It was hard not to be salty about the entire situation but I guess deep down inside, I always knew what things were between Azul and me. Our marriage was about business; I just hoped that with time, he would naturally fall in love as I did.

"A shooting between police and a twenty-seven-year-old man in East New York ended fatally. Another man, twenty-seven years old also, was critically injured and taken to Brookdale Hospital. We have no more updates at this time."

The newscaster on the television caught my attention, so I turned the volume up and paid attention. When the camera view panned out, it showed the entire street.

Crime scene tape circled around the corner in front of a Jamaican restaurant. There was a pool of blood on the concrete in front of it. As the camera panned from left to right, I paid attention to the cars and bystanders. That's when I noticed Azul's new car. I knew his license plate by heart and, as I repeated the plate numbers out loud, my eyes started to water.

Quickly, I dialed his number but it went straight to voicemail. I didn't know if he was the one that was dead or injured or if he had nothing to do with the situation at all. What I did know was that his car was parked at the fire hydrant with crime scene tape wrapped around it. My stomach fell into my ass as I wondered about his outcome. I called my uncle in a ball of tears. Just because Azul and I were no longer together didn't mean that I wanted anything to happen to him.

"Tío, something happened to Azul."

"I know my love, he's okay. His friend, the light-skinned one, should be there shortly."

My uncle made no effort to learn anyone's name. Before I could respond, David walked into my room. He was Azul's best man at our wedding. He seemed cool on the encounters that I had to be around him, but knowing that he was day ones with Azul meant that he was day ones with Justice. So, I knew where his loyalties lied.

"Tio, I'm going to call you back," I said into the phone as I watched my new guest saunter into the room.

One thing about David, he was comfortable wherever he went just like Azul. He sat in one of the seats that stood at my bedside.

"Azul got shot but he straight. You had my niece?"

Because I was freezing in my room, I had a sheet and two blankets covering me. He couldn't see that my belly was now as flat as a board. I was thankful for the instant snap

172

back. He said the news about Azul with no damn emotion. He needed a lesson in bedside manners.

"She's in the nursery," I finally answered.

He stood, and I thought that was rude as hell.

"Um... where are you going?" My perfectly arched eyebrow rose as I questioned him.

"To see her, duh."

I sucked my teeth because his boorish ass was irking me. Azul was rude as hell too, but he had some more suave to his slick-ass mouth. Before he exited my room, he stood in the doorway for a little minute before turning around to face me.

"How are you feeling though? After giving birth and shit?"

"I've seen better days."

He didn't even let me finish speaking before he walked out. I needed the time in the room by myself though, so it was whatever to me. I had nothing but time on my hands.

Through the course of my pregnancy between Lamaze classes, pampering myself, and putting together Aliana's nursery with the help of Azul, I had outlined the plan for my business. Now that baby girl was born, I was ready to execute all of the planning that I had done over the past seven months. I didn't know what Azul was into that brought harm his way, but it made me iffy about letting our daughter be alone with him. Having her made me realize that I was just now experiencing true love. Wouldn't anyone love me like my daughter, and her love was all that I needed. Her love and my business.

***

JUSTICE

6 MONTHS LATER...

I stood in the doorway of our house and held the door open for Azul. The rain outside was pouring down, and it was suitable to my mood. This was my first time being around his child and my nerves were bad. I watched, as he opened his car door, opened the umbrella, and grabbed the car seat from the rear of his truck. He closed the door and jogged lightly in my direction, so I held the door open wider for him and Aliana. I could hear her crying, as he stepped over our threshold. I closed the door behind him and grabbed the wet umbrella out of his hand.

"She's hungry," he said, as I closed the umbrella and placed it beside our front door.

He placed the car seat onto the floor and took the sixth-month-old out. I always knew that Aliana was Azul's twin, but seeing them side by side in person hurt me to my core. Her deep chocolate skin was identical to his. Dimples formed in her chubby cheeks as her cry echoed off the walls of our house. Her little noggin was filled with thick curly coils. Azul had been going over things with me for the past week. How many scoops of the formula go in the bottle and how I should rock my body to the side to get her to bed quickly. The shit was too much if you asked me. I was dealing with my own personal demons and this nigga wanted me to play step-mommy. Still, I watched some YouTube videos to help me. I reached my arms out for Aliana because I didn't want her to get sick from being pressed up against the wet material of Azul's shirt.

When the jewel on my finger glistened under the lights of our foyer, that's when I realized that I wasn't *playing* step mommy. I signed up for this shit, the GIA-certified, 3.14-carat purplish pink diamond engagement ring with the double halo wedding bands to match and the marriage license I had framed and hung on our bedroom wall was proof of that. Once Azul passed Aliana to me, all crying ceased to exist.

"She's not hungry; she just doesn't like ya ass." I looked down at her, and she gave me a gummy smile. "Ain't that right mama? We can't stand Daddy's ass."

I threw her over my shoulder and swayed from side to side just as he had taught me. I pushed my glasses up on my nose and watched as Azul pulled his t-shirt over his head. His toned midsection had me ready to toss the baby in my arms back into the car seat and ride his ass until the morning dew hit the grass in our front yard. Across the top of his stomach, my name was tatted in cursive. Right, where the E ended in Justice was the bullet wound that he would walk around with for the rest of his life. Just looking at that shit made me appreciate him still being here with me. I watched him walk towards the kitchen. Knowing that he was most likely going to fix a bottle for Aliana, I walked up the stairs with her.

In a matter of months, our master bedroom had transformed drastically. My clean modern décor was bombarded with a crib, baby toys, and whatnot. We had a spare bedroom just for Aliana, but Azul hated waking up out of sleep as is. So, I was sure that having to walk down the hall to tend to his daughter's needs in the middle of the night would frustrate him. Plus, he was a hard sleeper anyway, so I doubt that he would have even woken up from her crying in just the next room. He gave me full control to decorate her space as I pleased, and I couldn't wait until she was a little older so that I could see what she was interested in to make it the highlight of her room.

I took off Aliana's cute little Ralph Lauren jean jacket and placed her on the bed. I needed to get comfortable myself, so I took off my robe and went to hang it on the back of the bathroom door.

BOOM!

"Shit," I mumbled under my breath once her screams filled our bedroom. I dropped my robe on the bathroom floor and ran to get her tiny ass off the mocha-colored oak hardwood floor. It was my first time being around the damn baby, and she chose to be a damn acrobat and put all that crawling time to the test by diving head first off of our bed. I tried to shh her before Azul brought his ass upstairs in *daddy mode.*

CHAPTER 11

AZUL

I was nervous about Justice meeting Aliana in person. Seeing pictures and knowing that I now had a daughter was one thing, but to have the miniature version of me staring at her in the eyes was something else. This moment was what I had been waiting on for damn near six months. I had finally gotten Isabella to agree with me taking Aliana for the night. I guess the success with her salon and her uncomfortableness with leaving baby girl with a nanny was what made her soft to the idea of me taking her. I was blessed that she didn't hold any animosity for how things had ended with me and her. I knew that she knew that Justice wouldn't bring any harm to our child because of the love she had for me. Most niggas in my situation would have been dealing with drama out of the ass but, for the most part, I was straight.

I gathered a bottle for Aliana and grabbed the Enfamil out of one of the upper black cabinets. I was stuck in my thoughts on how Justice took control when I came through the door with baby girl. In my eyes, she was the shit. She was perfection, and I felt damn blessed to have her in my life. For example, a bottle warmer sat on the surface of one of our marble countertops, courtesy of her. Any and everything she could have purchased to make my life easier when it came to being a parent, she got. I opened a bottle of water and poured it into the bottle. I took a scoop out of the Enfamil can and prepared myself to put it into the bottle when a loud thud above my head made me drop the spoon and the formula all over the counter.

Aliana was screaming her head off, and I never heard her cry like that. My baby was crying like something was hurting her, and that made my long legs move with speed. I skipped two and three stairs at a time as I hurried to the second story of our home.

"What the fuck happened?"

I was out of breath by the time I reached our bedroom. Justice was slowly pacing back and forth as she held Aliana close to her chest.

"Shh... shh, you okay mama. You okay."

"What... the fuck happened?" this time, I said with heavy emphasis.

She turned my way quickly with an attitude plastered across her face like my damn kid wasn't screaming her head off. "Babies fall. I know you heard what the fuck happened. She's good; look, she's not even crying anymore."

I walked closer to them and saw that my baby's round eyes were just misted with tears and she was sniffling instead of screaming her head off. Her tiny hand was locked onto the spaghetti strap of Justice's shirt. I reached my arms out for her, but she nestled her head deeper into Justice's breasts.

"Exactly, now, leave us the fuck alone."

Justice walked over to our bed and took a seat. I didn't even think of how I must have offended her.

"I'm sorry, Ma."

I knew that she heard me because she had rolled those chinky eyes, but she didn't offer a response. I decided to go back downstairs and finish making Aliana's bottle to give Justice a moment to cool down. While I stood in the kitchen preparing the bottle, I heard Aliana's little laugh and, then, I heard Justice talking in her baby voice. I smiled because my gutta bitch was a blessing for sure.

"Zoo, hurry up!"

I heard Aliana starting to fuss, so I knew that's why Justice was rushing me. I quickly grabbed the bottle out of the warmer and skipped two and three stairs at a time to make it to the second level. When I got in the room, Aliana was down to her onesie and socks. Without having that motherly touch to her, Justice sure did move like an old-school mama. One thing about those old-school mamas was they were going to strip a baby as soon as they got inside the house.

Justice reached out with one hand while the other was throwing a receiving blanket over her shoulder. I just stood back lovingly and watched because I didn't even know where she had gotten all this shit from. I was showing her stupid shit like how Aliana liked to be rocked and I didn't think of all of this other shit that she was naturally doing. I handed her the bottle when she impatiently shook her hand my way.

She popped the lid off and temperature-checked the milk, and that shit made me want to put another seed up in her. I saw how quickly Aliana gravitated towards Justice and I loved that shit. Justice did a little rock, as Aliana drank from the bottle. I went to lie on the other side of the bed because honestly, a nigga was tired. With Isabella being so busy with her shop, I was the one doing all of the runarounds when it came to Aliana. As soon as I laid my back down on the bed and tried to close my eyes to get some rest, my phone vibrated in my pocket.

When I saw that it was Isabella Facetime calling me, I debated if I should answer or not. Justice holding Aliana closely while feeding her may have been too much for Isabella, but Justice was my wife now and Isabella was going to have to learn to respect that. The way I saw it was Isabella should have been grateful that there was someone extra in her daughter's life to love up on her. It's some stepmothers in this world that be bitter as shit. I done heard stories of bitches pinching babies and shit. I would put anyone in the dirt for the little girl that stole my heart as soon as I met her, even her own damn mother. I sighed before sliding the bar across my screen to answer. Isabella had her phone propped up on this stand because she was blowing out someone's hair.

"Not the boss doing work," I joked with her.

She pushed the Air Pods further into her ear. "This is my peace, you know?"

I did know. Everyone had their little thing that would ease their mind, and having her hand in somebody else's scalp was it for her.

"Where is my cupcake?" she asked as she turned off the blow dryer and placed it down.

"She's eating."

"Let me see her."

It could have just been me, but I hated that shit. Aliana was literally a baby; what the fuck enjoyment could she get out of watching her eat? I hesitated with flipping the camera but I did it anyway.

"Awww, bendito mami. Hey Justice…"

I looked at Justice, and she looked at me before she smiled and offered a response.

"Hey, Isabella."

Her stone wasn't the fake one that she had been putting on over the past months, and that made me smile. Isabella had been giving me hell since I got shot and she added a little more fire to her bullshit once Justice and I got married. The ladies seemed to be at peace and that's all that mattered in my life. The money was great and my family was better.

"Well, call me back before bedtime so that she can hear my voice before she sleeps."

"Aight," I said to Isabella before ending the call.

I had to give it to her. She was a damn good mother. At this young age, our daughter was already sleeping through the night and she had a bedtime. I placed my phone on the nightstand and turned to face my wife and daughter. I watched Justice lightly pat Aliana on the back to get her to burp.

"Ahh, big burp little mamas."

Her baby voice was cute as fuck. Growing up, I would have thought that Justice would have been talking to babies on some 50 Cent gangsta shit, but this girl was over there with the Elmo voice, and Aliana was loving it. I needed a moment to rest my eyes, and I knew that Aliana was in great hands. With Justice at my side, I knew that she would be in great hands for the rest of her life.

***

JUSTICE

I exhaled the smoke from my nose and mouth as I sat on the balcony. Azul and Aliana were sound asleep and, as I watched them through the glass sliding door, I smiled slightly. Never in a million years would I think that I would find so much happiness in what was actually a fucked up ass situation. You never realized how bad someone had treated you until you said that shit out loud and, when I got down to telling the story between me and Azul, the shit sounded horrible. If you asked me by listening to my own story, the only upside to the entire shit was the money that had crossed through my hands and the status that came with being a drug dealer's wife.

For nine years, I was a soldier, a rider, a gutta bitch, a side bitch and, for the last almost two, I became a housewife. Of course, I had my moments when I missed being carefree, ruthless, and just a gangsta. I was reformed now. Still, I was indeed that bitch. I had just learned a lot and, through experience, I had changed for the better.

I quickly ashed the tip to my blunt and sat it in the ashtray when I started to see Ali moving around. I had given her that little nickname because I could tell that when she got older, she was gonna have some spice to her. Putting her in boxing classes was at the top of my list if that was okay with her parents of course. I sprayed myself with some Febreze before sliding the glass door and entering our bedroom.

When we first moved into this house, I expressed the importance of a balcony in our bedroom just so that I could get fucked on it and, now, here I was using what was supposed to be my nasty space as a getaway just to take one to the face. As soon as Aliana started a slight whimper, Azul opened his eyes and grabbed her into his arm.

"Mrs. Jones, come lay next to a nigga."

His hood ass, I thought to myself as I smirked. I stepped out of my house shoes and found a comfortable spot on the other side of him. Once my head laid on his chest, he wrapped his arm around me. Lightly, he kissed my forehead.

"I love you…" he said lowly, I was sure not to wake Aliana.

"Love you more."

I nestled my head deeper into his armpit as I let my eyes take the rest that was very much needed. Our story wasn't for most, but it was for us and I was at peace with every decision I had made since meeting Azul Jones. I made a mental note to remind him of the upcoming drop we had. Yeah, I took on the title of housewife full fledge but wouldn't shit keep me away from the game, and I loved that Azul respected that about me. Wasn't shit better than having ya nigga understand and embrace who you truly are and, although the ride with Zoo has been crazy, I don't regret a damn thing.

THE END

ABOUT THE AUTHOR

C. Wilson was born in Bedford-Stuyvesant, Brooklyn, New York. Publishing her first book in 2016, she continued to perfect her craft. *A Summer in Miami* is one of her most talked about books. She allows her readers to escape reality for a brief moment and, when they are back, they are left with an enjoyable feeling. There are gems in her pages and trust, you will indeed find a "book bae".

What's next for C. Wilson?

Expect book appearances, conferences, public appearances, and, of course, more fiction novels.

AWARDS:

UBAWA's Top 100 Authors of 2018

My Boozie Book Club's December 2019 Author of the Month

Bookednboujee's Top 100 Books of 2019 #19 Love in-between the White Lines 1

NOMINATIONS:

UBAWA's Top 100 Authors of 2019

To keep up with everything C. Wilson, subscribe to her mailing list at

www.authorcwilson.com

FOR AUTOGRAPHED COPIES VISIT:

www.authorcwilson.com

OTHER BOOKS BY AUTHOR

Truth is Stranger than Fiction 1-2

Love in-between the White Lines 1-3

A Love Affair for Eternity 1-4

Love in-between Eternity's Holiday

From Paris with Love

Saved by a Down South Savage

A Summer in Miami

I'm Giving Myself Over to You

Melanin Mama: A Self-Care Journal for Black Women

The Twelve Days of Christmas: A Christmas Erotica

I Want a Taste

Dear Diary: The Deanna Dixon Story 1-2

Made in the USA
Columbia, SC
24 June 2024

37368920R00117